The fear was so strong, it choked her.

Forcing herself to shake it off, she focused on fixing dinner. But when another officer approached Miles, putting something on the table, she froze. He looked up, his face full of dread. "Rebecca, no," he signed. He spoke to the officer, gesturing at a wrinkled picture on the table.

Lipreading had never been her forte. For the first time she wished it was.

What was in that picture that had Miles so shook up?

She stepped closer to get a look...and her world tilted. Bile surged in her throat, choking off her breath. The glass slipped from her fingers, shattering.

"That picture was in a frame on my desk," she signed to Miles. "It was taken last year."

His arms tightened around her. Despite the comfort they offered, she'd never forget the image of her and her friends laughing at the camera. Or the red *X* slashed through her friend's face.

And the circle around her own.

She understood the message. Her friend was dead... and she was next.

Dana R. Lynn grew up in Illinois. She met her husband at a wedding and told her parents she had met her future husband. Nineteen months later, they were married. Today they live in rural Pennsylvania with their three children, two dogs, one cat, one rabbit, one horse and six chickens. In addition to writing, she works as an educational interpreter for the deaf and is active in several ministries in her church.

Books by Dana R. Lynn

Love Inspired Suspense

Amish Country Justice

Plain Target
Plain Retribution

Presumed Guilty
Interrupted Lullaby

Visit the Author Profile page at Harlequin.com.

PLAIN RETRIBUTION

DANA R. LYNN

HARLEQUIN® LOVE INSPIRED® SUSPENSE

Recycling programs
for this product may
not exist in your area.

LOVE INSPIRED BOOKS

ISBN-13: 978-0-373-67840-2

Plain Retribution

Copyright © 2017 by Dana Roae

www.Harlequin.com

Printed in U.S.A.

What shall we then say to these things?
If God be for us, who can be against us?
–Romans 8:31

This book is dedicated to my family, who supported me through all the craziness. Love you. And to my Lord, in awe of His many blessings.

Acknowledgments:

Thank you so much to everyone who helped with this book. To my friends in the Deaf community, thank you for helping me to get into my heroine's head and understand her better. To Shelley Shepard Gray, thanks for sharing your experience and love of the Amish community. It made such a difference! To my critique partners and friends, thank you for reading and pointing out problems, lending a shoulder to cry on, or just sharing a cup of coffee and letting me vent.

Thanks to my editor, Elizabeth Mazer, and Love Inspired Books for all the hard work and support. You are amazing and I am so grateful for the opportunity to work with you.

A special thanks to my agent, Tamela Hancock Murray. Even though you are not the agent of record for this book, your advice and friendship have been invaluable.

Special thanks to my late agent, Mary Sue Seymour, a wonderful mentor and friend.

ONE

She hated this time of night.

Rebecca Miller stepped outside and shut the shop's door behind her, taking care to lock it. The air was thick with the smell of wood smoke from the houses nearby. She rubbed her arms to ward off a chill—not all of it from the cool fall air. The hair on the back of her neck prickled. Was she being watched? Holding the key out in front of her like a weapon, she peered into the darkness. Nothing. Her brother Levi would have cautioned her against letting her imagination run wild. Her Amish mother would chide her for her lack of faith in the Lord's protection. Well, she had faith. But she had also learned the hard way that having faith did not prevent horrible things from happening. And she had the scars, mentally and physically, to prove it.

Her breathing quickened. She forced herself to breathe slowly. In. Out. In. Out. Better. Was she panting? Could anyone hear it?

Levi had told her that hearing people could hear the sound of her rapid breaths when she was frightened. How accurate that was, she didn't know. She'd never heard breathing, or any other sound, in her entire life. Rebecca had been profoundly deaf since she had been born into her large Amish family. They hadn't put hearing aids on her. When she had left her Amish community instead of being baptized at seventeen, she had tried them, but didn't notice any difference. Now at twenty-five, she had no interest in trying them again.

She rarely allowed her deafness to hold her back, having spent years striving for independence in the hearing world, but sometimes she felt the lack of hearing keenly. Like now, knowing if someone was stepping closer to her, she'd never hear them coming.

She wondered again what had possessed her to agree—for the first time since she'd taken the job—to close by herself the bookstore she worked in. Every other time she'd worked this late, she'd had someone else closing with her. Granted, it was only a little after eight thirty in the evening, but in October, it was so dark out that it might as well have been ten o'clock at night. She shivered. Whether from cold or apprehension, she wasn't sure.

Sucking in a deep breath for fortification, she

started across the empty alley to where her car was parked. Maybe she should have taken her best friend Jess's offer to let her husband, Seth, drive her home when he had finished his work shift. She could have waited inside the locked store until he came, and they could have retrieved her car tomorrow. Not wanting to put them out, she'd refused. Now she wished she'd accepted.

No. She shook her head. It was time she took care of herself and got over her fear of the dark.

In her periphery, a shadow moved. She flinched. *You're being ridiculous*, she signed in her head. No one was there.

Her heart continued to thud inside her chest. Memories of the past started to cloud her thoughts. What if someone was out there, like before? Only, this time, she was alone. Of course, having people with her hadn't been enough to protect her back then.

Please, Lord, be my shield.

Holding her hand out, she pressed the key fob to unlock the car door. The headlights blinked, then remained on. In the sudden light, she saw her hand was shaking. She hated the fear that crawled inside her. The fear that kept her from going about her life like anyone else. Instead, she was constantly looking over her shoulder.

Just a few more feet, and she would be safe

inside her car. She quickened her pace and practically threw herself into the car, then slammed the door behind her. Leaning back against the headrest, she let out a slow breath and felt her heart pounding inside her chest.

Remaining where she was, she flicked her gaze to the rearview mirror. And froze.

Cold, dark eyes glittered at her from beneath a dark ski mask. Someone was in her car!

Whipping around, she came face-to-face with a nightmare. The intruder shot forward and grabbed her by the neck and yanked her back against the headrest, trying to choke her. She couldn't breathe! Lungs burning, the keys fell from her hand as she twisted and turned, trying to break her attacker's hold. Both of her hands latched on to the arm around her throat. She tugged and pulled with all her might, but to no avail. Her eyes seemed hyperfocused, zooming in on every detail as adrenaline coursed through her system. She saw every hair on the arm that tightened around her throat, noted the sharp lines of the tattoo on his wrist. She struggled against her attacker's grip, but he wouldn't budge. Her knee banged against the steering wheel. She barely noticed it.

The alley was empty. There was no use hoping anyone would see her.

The man's grip tightened. Rebecca clawed

at his arm as hard as she could, feeling several fingernails break off. Lifting one hand, she shoved it back into the attacker's face, stabbing her thumb into one dark eye.

The black-masked figure reared back and rubbed his injured eye.

She was free! But she wasn't safe. Not yet.

Before the villain could recover, Rebecca fumbled for the door latch and tumbled out of the car. Gaining her feet, she bolted.

Out into the alley and toward Main Street, she ran as fast as her long legs would carry her.

As she approached the end of the alley, the glow from the streetlights cast shadows on the buildings she raced past. The attacker's shadow loomed too close. And it was getting closer. Her attacker was only a few feet behind her! Leaning forward, she pushed herself harder.

A hand slid down her hair. She felt a few strands catch, rip out of her scalp. The pain was instant, but it wasn't enough to stop her. She kept running, even as her eyes watered.

She opened her mouth. She screamed. Whether it was loud enough for anyone to hear, she had no idea. But her throat was raw. And her energy was waning.

Almost there.

Her attacker grabbed her from behind and threw her to the ground. Rebecca skidded onto the ground. Gravel scraped across her palms, and she ripped her skirt.

She flipped herself over to a sitting position so she could see her assailant. As he rushed toward her again, she scooped up a handful of dirt and gravel and flung it at the disguised figure with all her might. Her aim was true.

There was a brief moment of satisfaction as he covered his eyes with his gloved hands. But she knew this wouldn't hold him off for long, so she didn't hang around to gloat. She jumped to her feet and ran out into the street.

And right into the path of a moving car.

The car veered slightly to the side and came to a sudden halt inches from hitting her.

Praise the Lord. She sent up an earnest prayer. It was a police car. She had almost been run down by one of LaMar Pond's finest. And now she had an officer to protect her from the attacker, who had to be closing in on her by now.

Shooting a panicked glance over her shoulder, she exhaled in relief when she saw her attacker had fled.

The police car door opened and a tall officer jumped from the vehicle and rushed to her side. He pulled her off the street and onto the sidewalk, under a streetlight. For the first time, she took note of his familiar features. Warm blue eyes, blond hair that tended to get shaggy.

Miles Olsen. She sighed in relief. She had met the young officer last spring when Jess had been in danger. Not only was he a policeman, but he was also the only one in LaMar Pond who could sign.

"Rebecca! I almost hit you. What's wrong?" Miles signed to her in fluent ASL.

"You didn't see him?" she signed back.

He immediately straightened and peered into the alley she had just exited. "Was someone bothering you?"

"He attacked me. He was waiting in my car. I didn't notice until I'd already gotten in..."

She couldn't go on. The trembling started inside and worked itself outward until she was shaking so hard she could barely stand up.

A strong arm wrapped around her shoulder and led her back to the police car. Miles ushered her into the passenger side of the car then reached past her to flip on the hazard lights and grab a flashlight. He switched on the light and shone it back down the alley. Which, as far as she could see, was empty.

Activating the radio hooked to his shoulder, he said something into it. "I called for backup. It should be here soon," he signed to her when he finished. "You stay here. I'm going to lock the car and have a look around."

Rebecca started to protest. She didn't want

to be a sitting duck all by herself if her attacker came back. Plus, the idea of being alone was terrifying right now. She wondered if this was what people meant when they talked about going into shock. It was hard to wrap her mind around what was happening.

Miles squatted, putting them on the same level with each other. Switching the flashlight to his left hand, he continued to sign with his right. "Don't worry. I will wait to canvas your car until help arrives. But I need to make sure he isn't hiding out nearby. I'll stay in sight. Okay?"

It made sense. As long as she could see him, there was no reason to panic.

She nodded. Miles swung the door closed. Placing her hand on the door panel, she felt the vibration of the locking mechanism sliding into place. Only then did she relax. Craning her neck, she watched Miles cautiously approach the alley and inspect it for hidden threats.

Several cars passed them. The flashing lights inside the dark car made her imagine shadows that weren't there. *Hurry, please*, she thought.

Five minutes later, he jogged back to the car and let himself in.

"I didn't see anything suspicious. I still need to examine your car. But I don't want to leave you here by yourself. Let me check on the status of our backup, and we can get this sorted out."

She nodded to show she understood.

Using the button on the dashboard, he placed the call. "They'll be here in a minute," he assured her, then turned off the hazard lights and moved his vehicle over to the side of the street. "I also called for the paramedics. Your throat looks bruised."

She grimaced, but didn't argue. Her throat was hurting.

He reached down for a notebook and a pen. "Okay," he signed. "I need you to tell me everything you can remember. Start at the beginning."

Sitting forward, she closed her eyes as she racked her brain to figure out the sequence of events. It was easier to focus on what had occurred if she wasn't looking at him.

"I work at A Novel Idea. I had agreed to close alone tonight. We stay open late on Wednesday nights. My boss, April Long, was going to visit her parents for a few days, or she would have closed with me, the way she usually does. I walked to my car, got in, looked into the rearview mirror—"

Abruptly, she stopped. The memory of those cold eyes glaring back at her had icy fingers running up and down her spine. She dropped her head into her trembling hands.

A hand tapping her left shoulder jolted her

out of her fear. Moving her head so her cheek rested on her clasped hands, she glanced over at the cop.

"It's okay," he signed. "I know this is hard, but we'll figure this out."

Breaking eye contact, he sent a cursory glance down at the notes he had made. "So, did anyone else know what time you were leaving tonight?"

Tilting her head, Rebecca sucked her bottom lip into her mouth and chewed on it.

"I don't know. It's been on the schedule all week. Oh, I did tell one person—I was emailing Jess yesterday about something else, and mentioned that I'd be closing. She offered to have Seth drive me, but I told her I'd be okay." She pushed back her hair and plowed through the rest. "He was waiting for me inside my car. Tried to choke me. I stabbed him in the eye and tried to escape. But he caught me again."

Forcing herself to sign slowly and precisely, she described the attack.

"If you hadn't shown up when you did, he would have gotten me."

She could have died. Been kidnapped. Robbed. Beaten. Any number of horrible things could have happened to her.

Miles shoved away the anger that was burning in his gut, tamping it down so it wouldn't show on his face. She'd been through a traumatic experience and he didn't want to scare her.

He didn't know the woman sitting next to him that well. She was close to Jess McGrath, now Jess Travis, and he knew that she and her family had helped Jess and Miles's friend Seth when they'd been in danger last spring. Thankfully, the ordeal had had a happy ending, with Jess and Seth managing to unmask their attackers—while falling in love with each other in the process.

They'd gotten married not long ago, and Rebecca had been at the wedding, as had Miles. He had even been asked to interpret for her and several other guests who were deaf or hard of hearing, like Rebecca and Jess. He'd assumed, since her brother was Amish, that Rebecca must have been at one time. But he had never tried to find out more. He'd ignored the initial spark of attraction he had experienced when he'd first met her, when Jess had been under attack. It hadn't been the appropriate time or place. Plus, he couldn't afford to mess up another case with his rash actions.

By the time the case had been closed, he'd convinced himself it was best to keep his distance. Sure, he could have found where she lived, or asked Jess for a way to contact her. But he had let the opportunity slip away. And anyway, she hadn't shown any interest in him.

No, he didn't know her well, but it bothered him when a young woman was victimized. He needed to be careful. He'd let himself act upon his anger once before when involved in a case, and it had almost ruined his career. Even though that time it was personal. Very personal. Couldn't fall into that trap again. He was still trying to get back into his chief's good graces.

He asked her a few more questions, trying to get most of the details down while they were waiting.

Red and blue flashing lights caught his attention. A second police cruiser pulled up in front of his, then shifted back to parallel-park against the curb. Good. Jackson was here. And he hadn't come in hot. Lights, but no siren. If the attacker was still hanging around, there was nothing to cue him that backup had arrived.

"Okay. Sergeant Jackson is here. I'll have him start looking at your car while we finish this."

Miles opened his door and stepped out. Turning to Rebecca, he paused and took in her wide blue eyes and troubled face. At least her cheeks seemed to have some color, and her trembling had ceased. She looked calmer. Actually, she looked beautiful. If he hadn't met her previously, he would not have guessed her background, growing up Amish. Her skirt was long, but it was rust-colored with gold, brown and orange leaves on it. It was pretty on her. He pressed his lips together when his gaze fell on the rip at her knee. Her gold sweater was simple but elegant. Her pale hair was shorter than he remembered, ending just an inch or two below her shoulders. It made him think of summer, the way it shimmered gold.

What? That kind of thinking would get him nowhere.

"Olsen, what do ya know?" Gavin Jackson sauntered toward him. His voice was casual, friendly, but his gaze was in constant motion, sweeping the area for any threats. Keeping it concise, Miles brought him up to speed.

"Rebecca Miller? Hey, I remember her from Travis's wedding. Cute little thing." Jackson ducked down to wave at the girl sitting in the car. Miles frowned, not sure why it bothered him to see Jackson smiling at her. But it did.

"Okay, Casanova. Let's process the scene."

Jackson's brows rose, but he made no comment about Miles telling a higher ranking officer what to do. Instead, the man shrugged and shifted back into cop mode.

Between the two of them, they managed to get the scene processed in a relatively short time. Miles kept a close eye on Rebecca. She had refused to sit in the car by herself. To be honest, he preferred having her where he could keep an eye on her. By herself, she wouldn't be able to hear the attacker return. And even though having her accompany them meant she was out in the open, exposed to another attack, it was hardly likely that her assailant would come back with two officers so close.

When the paramedics arrived, Miles jogged over to interpret for her briefly. He knew the paramedic in charge, a serious blonde woman named Sydney.

Not surprisingly, Rebecca refused to go to the hospital. Sydney didn't push the issue.

"There's no bulging around the area. And your color looks good," Sydney told her as Miles interpreted. "If you have any trouble breathing or opening your mouth, or if swallowing becomes painful, you need to go to the ER. Immediately."

Rebecca nodded and thanked the woman.

Miles returned to Jackson.

Now they just needed to finish looking over the car, checking to be sure it hadn't been sabotaged. It was a possibility. Even in the light of day, the alley behind the store was empty. Only businesses. And most of the businesses closed at five. Chances were good that anyone could damage the car without fear of getting caught.

Inside the car, there were no prints, no clues left behind. The attacker had been careful. Except that the back locks had been jimmied. Something was lying on the floorboard. Flashing a light in that direction, he saw Rebecca's purse. It had been knocked over, the contents spilled everywhere. Why didn't women use bags that zipped? Seeing her phone, he snatched it up and brought it to her.

"Do you have anyone you can call tonight? Someone to stay with you?"

She nodded. It bothered him to see her so pale and worn. Even her signs were lackluster. "My roommate will be home later. She works until ten. She usually arrives home around eleven."

"Maybe send her a text. Let her know what happened so she'll know to come straight home." He handed her the phone, then left her while she composed the text.

"Pop the hood," Jackson called, scooting out from his position under the car.

Miles jogged around to the driver's side and leaned in to pull the lever. The hood released with a small click.

Jackson whistled.

"What?" Miles stepped up beside his colleague. "Wow."

The engine had been incapacitated, the spark plugs nowhere to be found. One thing was clear—whoever had attacked Rebecca had wanted to be sure she couldn't get away.

"Do you think she was specifically targeted?" He took out his cell phone and snapped pictures of the engine. "Could this be random?"

His gut told him no. This kind of attention to detail took forethought and planning.

Jackson was already shaking his head, frowning.

"I don't think so."

"I don't, either." Miles shoved his hands in his pockets, watching Rebecca as she sat on the cement curb. She looked tuckered out. No wonder. "How does this play for you? I think the perp has been watching her for some time. Maybe a few days, maybe longer. It's possible he picked her because she was deaf. Thought she'd be an easy mark. He knows where she leaves her car, and what hours she works. Chances are he waited here for her."

"But if April hadn't left early, he would have had to contend with two women."

Jackson had a point. He went to Rebecca and posed the question. A minute later he was back.

"Not necessarily. Rebecca said April usually parked in the parking garage across the street. All he would have needed to do was stay down until she was out of sight." He rubbed the back of his neck.

The quiet was broken with a ridiculously raucous ringtone coming from his watch. Jackson's brows rose in amusement. Miles brought up his wrist and fumbled with the buttons, mumbling an apology. He'd left his earpiece in the car, so he moved slightly away from Jackson. It was the chief.

"Olsen here."

"Report, Officer Olsen," the chief of police ordered.

"Sir, the perp is gone and has left no traces we could find. He disabled the car, though. It needs to be towed. Jackson and I think he's been watching Rebecca for a while."

"Rebecca?" There wasn't any censure in the chief's tone, just mild curiosity.

"Sorry, sir. Miss Miller. I know her. Anyhow, we don't yet know why she was targeted."

"Ahh." He could picture the chief nodding as he leaned back in his swivel chair. "Even if the perp was watching her, it might have still been a random attack. Maybe he noticed she drove alone and parked in the alley and thought she looked like an easy mark."

"Sir, I'm going to drive Miss Miller home, and then come in and file paperwork."

"Very well. Does she have someone she could stay with?"

Miles cast a concerned glance toward her. Her arms were crossed on the top of her knees, and her head was down.

"Miles?"

Huh? Oh, right.

"Yes. She has a roommate. I had her text the woman and let her know what was going on."

"Good. I'm glad she'll have someone there for her," the chief responded in a smooth drawl.

Miles thought for a second, deciding his next move. "I also think we should try to get the visual artist in as soon as she's available to see if she can remember any details that might get some hits on the database. Oh, and see if the interpreter is available."

"If not, you could interpret if she waives her right to a certified interpreter."

Miles frowned. "Yes, sir. Although I think it would be better to have someone certified."

People didn't always understand that managing direct communication in sign language and interpreting at a professional level were two totally different skills. Just because someone could speak the language didn't mean they could expertly translate it into English.

"I agree. But interpreters are very hard to come by."

"Yes, sir. I will try to get all that scheduled ASAP."

"Sounds like a good plan." A pause. "Miles, I'm going to put you in charge of this case."

"Sir?" His heart thumped in his chest.

"You've been doing good work since you came back. I want to find this perp. And I think you've proven you can handle the responsibility. Plus, you can communicate directly with our victim, so that makes you the natural candidate."

"Thank you. I will do my best."

He tapped the face of the watch, disconnecting the call, joy bursting through his body. His first case as the lead. The chief trusted him again—he could finally put his past mistakes behind him. This had been a long time coming.

Then he looked at Rebecca, and some of the joy faded. As proud as he was to be lead in the case, he hated the idea that his victory came with the price of her horrible attack.

She was so vulnerable. Just like his stepsister, Sylvie, had been. Suppose this wasn't a one-time attack? Suppose the perp was a stalker, fixated on Rebecca? He would have his work cut out for him, finding the perp before he struck again. Oh, he'd been in on tough investigations before. Chief Paul Kennedy had been slowly giving him more and more responsibility as he had shown he could be relied on.

For some reason, though, this responsibility seemed heavier. Because it was quite likely that the beautiful young woman sitting a few feet away was still in danger.

TWO

The trip to Rebecca's apartment was a quiet one. She'd given him the address, and off they went. Since he was familiar with the area, he didn't need to take the time to plug the address into his GPS.

The trip was silent, but not uncomfortable. Rebecca had calmed down. Once they were ensconced in his vehicle and moving away from the scene, the tension in her shoulders and face seemed to have eased. She wasn't happy, but neither was she panicked. Which was good.

As for Miles, he appreciated the silence. It gave him a chance to process the events of the evening and get a hold of his own emotions. He couldn't help but worry about how she was handling the pressure, though. He turned to look at her—her expression was smooth, unruffled. Could she really be that calm? He would have expected more panic, or at least signs of discomfort. He'd seen the bruises on her neck—they had to be hurting.

Get a grip, Olsen. She's not your sister. She's strong. And now she's your case. Keep it professional.

He was so involved in his own thoughts, he almost missed the entrance to her apartment complex. Good thing Windy Hill Apartments had a large sign out by the road. Grimacing, he shifted on his blinker and spun the wheel at the last second, swerving hard into the driveway. In his periphery, he saw Rebecca put her hand on the dashboard to brace herself.

Bet that impressed her. Not.

What an awful parking lot to come into at night. It had one light, right in front of the entrance. But the rest was dark, the corners in the lot merging into the shadows and trees. Anyone could hide out in those shadows, and she wouldn't be aware of it until it was too late. Rebecca wouldn't be able to hear any telltale sounds that might warn her of impending danger.

Great. Now he was getting paranoid on her behalf.

He parked the cruiser under the light and switched off the ignition. Turning to face Rebecca, he paused when he saw her pensive glance. Her eyebrows squished together and her lips tightened. She flickered her gaze around the dark edges of the lot. Obviously, he wasn't the only one who found the place unsettling.

He tapped her on the shoulder once, to get her attention.

She glanced nervously at him. She was definitely disturbed by something.

"What's wrong?" he signed, folding his three middle fingers down over his palm while extending his thumb and little finger, then tapping the folded part against his chin.

She pointed to a window on the second floor. The curtains were open, and the lights were out. "That's my apartment. My roommate isn't home yet." Using the one-handed ASL alphabet, she finger-spelled her roommate's name. Holly Fletcher. "I knew she wouldn't be, but—"

"You are nervous about entering an empty apartment?" He raised his eyebrows and crooked the index finger of his right hand in a question mark.

"Yes."

She didn't look happy about admitting it. But at least she wasn't denying it.

"No problem. I will walk up with you and make sure it's all clear."

Nodding, she turned from him to get out of the car. But not before he saw the relieved smile that swept over her face.

Wow, she sure was pretty. Yeah, so not going there. Even though she was.

Back to work, Miles. You have a job to do. And then you need to leave.

Shoving those dangerous thoughts from his mind, he focused on the task at hand. He waited as she tapped in the five-digit entry code. Although not foolproof, the added security measure did make him feel better about her safety here. They climbed the single flight of stairs and walked to her apartment. When Rebecca moved to unlock the door, Miles held out a hand to stop her. Startled, she moved her gaze to his, her brows rising in a question.

"Give me your keys," he signed.

She dropped them in his open palm. He motioned for her to move back. As soon as she was away from the door, he leaned closer to listen for movement inside the apartment. Nothing. He unlocked the door as quietly as he could and signed for her to wait while he checked out the apartment. Her eyes widened as he removed his gun from the holster.

"Just a precaution," he signed.

Keeping his weapon at the ready, he moved through the apartment, checking each room. The kitchen was spotless. No sign of any disturbance. The first bedroom was clear. It was clean, like the kitchen, but he knew at once it was the friend's room rather than Rebecca's. Pictures of the attractive brunette with a hodge-podge of people and in a variety of settings covered the large corkboard on the wall, with some in frames on the desk and dresser.

The next room was obviously Rebecca's. The contrast was startling. The room was clean, but the decor was sparse. There were a couple of pictures. They all looked very recent, none dating back earlier than four or five years ago. And why would there be? The Amish didn't take pictures. Against the far wall, there was a large oil painting. It clearly showed a white farmhouse with a black Amish buggy in the front. It was so realistic, it looked like someone could reach out and open the door of the buggy. He peered closer to see the artist's signature, then whistled softly. Rebecca Miller. Wow. She had some mad talent.

On the desk under the window was an open laptop and several textbooks. A GED certificate was prominently displayed on the wall. That's right, he thought. The Amish only go to school through eighth grade. Right next to that was a college diploma. She had a bachelor's degree in art. It was awarded this past spring.

Giving in to his curiosity, Miles peered closer at the books. They covered topics ranging from the deaf community to the study of ASL and ethics and practices with interpreting for the deaf. Rebecca apparently aspired to get a CDI certificate. He'd only ever met one Certified Deaf Interpreter. They were highly sought after in improving communication with the deaf community in official settings. Good for her.

Returning to the living room, he found Rebecca standing inside the door, her back against the living room wall. Made sense. If you couldn't hear, you didn't want to leave yourself vulnerable to attacks from behind. Again.

"Nothing here. Are you sure you're all right? I can stay until your roommate gets back."

She was shaking her head before his hands stopped moving. "I'm fine. Thank you so much for checking. I feel silly, but I appreciate it."

He stepped closer to her and put his hand on hers to stop the apology, then pulled his hand back at the zing that shot up his arm. Her shocked expression told him all he needed to know. She had felt it, too, and by the look of the frown stamped on her pretty features, wasn't any happier about it than he was. Good. That meant she wouldn't expect anything. He ignored the twinge of disappointment.

He couldn't afford to get emotionally involved with anyone. Emotions had almost cost him his job once. In the end, he had kept his job, but had lost his rank as sergeant. That fact was brought home every time he put on his uniform without the insignia. All he wanted was to earn it back.

"I don't mind checking. I wanted to make sure you were safe." He looked at his watch. "It's almost ten now. Your roommate should be here in an hour. Let's trade numbers, and you can text me if you need anything. I'll text you to let you know if we have any leads."

They exchanged phones. He put in his number, then snapped a selfie so that she'd have a visual in her contacts. Oh, wait. Amish. He flicked a glance in her direction. She was shaking her head at him, a half smirk forming on her lips. Her face had more color in it now, he was glad to note. Her earlier pallor had bothered him.

"Sorry." He shrugged. "I can delete the picture if you want me to. I wasn't thinking."

"It's okay." She snapped a selfie of herself on his phone. "I'm not Amish anymore."

Amused, he chuckled. She was absolutely adorable. He took back his phone and synced it with his watch.

"I have never met anyone who left the Amish community before," he signed. Then he wondered if that statement bordered on rude. Although, bluntness was all part and parcel of deaf culture, so maybe she'd take it in stride.

She shrugged, her face rueful. "Not many do.

It was a tough decision, but in the end it was for the best." She shifted her eyes past him, thinking. "I was the only deaf person in my family. My parents are great, but they never really learned to sign fluently. ASL is a hard language to learn, and there weren't that many opportunities for them to learn it in the community. They speak Pennsylvania Dutch and English at home. I was caught between three languages. Out of my family, only my brother Levi and my sister Lizzy can really sign to me. In my classes every day, I'd have a few people I could speak with easily, but then I'd come home and have to struggle to understand and be understood. It grew worse after I left school. There were no interpreters. I think my parents accepted my leaving because they knew that I didn't even understand what was happening at church. In the English world, though, I could be part of the deaf community. I had friends, and I was able to be a full participant."

He nodded. "My grandparents and uncle are deaf. They are very involved with the deaf community."

"So that's why you sign so well! I had wondered."

"Yeah. I grew up with it." He tilted his head. "Do you regret leaving?"

"No. I love my family, and I am grateful to

still have a relationship with them. In fact, my oldest brother, Levi, is getting married in a week. On Thursday. I will be there. But someday, I want to get married, and I want my husband to be able to communicate with me. And if I have deaf children, I want them to have full access to the deaf community." She moved away a couple of feet. Restless. "Want to know what was really sad? Until a few years ago, I never even knew that Amish children say '*mam* and *dat*,' instead of 'mom and dad.'" She fingerspelled the Amish versions of the words. "I've never been good at lipreading, and wasn't able to really see the difference when I watched my siblings say the words. In my head, I always see the sign for 'mother and father,' but when I wrote, I wrote 'mom and dad.' Like the other kids at school. Levi read something I had written a few years back and pointed it out to me. He also took the time to teach me the written words and meanings of some of the other Amish words that were used daily, but that I never knew. I have taken pains to try to think of them as *mam* and *dat*, knowing that's how they would prefer to be called, but it wasn't automatic for me."

The urge to touch her hand, to offer comfort, sneaked up on him. He resisted. But it was difficult. The aloneness emanating from her posture as she signed just about killed him.

She's not alone now, he reminded himself. *She has friends in the deaf community. She has her faith. And her family does love her.*

And she has me.

No. She doesn't. I'm temporary. And I have stayed too long.

Lifting his wrist, he eyed the time on his digital watch. And whistled. It was later than he had thought.

"I need to go. Text me if you need anything," he signed with one hand, pocketing the phone. "And lock the door behind you."

She rolled her eyes, but complied without comment.

The second she had closed and locked the door, he was on his way to the station. It would take him twenty minutes to get there. If he worked fast, he should be able to have all his reports filed and all his duties completed by the time his shift ended at midnight. Unless, of course, another call came in. Wednesday nights were usually pretty quiet in LaMar Pond. He should be good.

An hour and a half later, he finished his reports.

With his work completed, his mind turned back to Rebecca. Had her roommate arrived home yet? Maybe he should send her a text to check on her. He quickly shot off a text.

Then he occupied himself while pretending he wasn't watching for a responding text. None came. No doubt her roommate had returned. She was no longer alone. Wilting back against his seat, he let out a sigh. It was after eleven thirty. Chances were good that she was asleep, or that she and her roommate were talking about the night's events and not paying attention to the phone.

Everything was fine.

But it wouldn't hurt to check on her in the morning, just to be sure.

Rebecca came awake with a start, heart pounding. Her hands flew to her throat—she could still feel hands closing around it. But as awareness seeped back in, she realized it was just a dream. No one was attacking her. She sat up, knocking a pillow off the couch in the process. A wave of dizziness attacked her. Closing her eyes, she breathed in deeply until the dizziness passed. When she could open her eyes again, she frowned. She was still in her skirt from work. She had fallen asleep after texting with her brother.

He didn't have a phone, so she had used the videophone to call one of her parents' neighbors who had agreed to let Rebecca's family know what had happened and that she was fine. Which had resulted in a long conversation with her brother. It took some doing, but she finally convinced him that she was okay and didn't need anyone to come to LaMar Pond.

A quick glance at the clock showed it was just past six in the morning.

She hadn't intended to spend the night on the couch. Why had Holly let her sleep? Her roommate usually woke her up if she fell asleep there. The couch was for sitting, not for sleeping. Holly had very definite views about that. So why change?

Rebecca stood and groaned as her back protested. Good grief, she was twenty-five, not seventy-five. She smiled at her silliness, then turned toward the bedrooms.

And every trace of her smile was wiped from her face.

Holly's door was wide open. As if Holly wasn't home.

Fear in her throat, Rebecca moved on leaden feet to the bedroom and flicked on the light.

The bed was made. Not a thing was out of place. The room was perfect. It made Rebecca's blood run cold.

Holly had never come home.

Her phone! There could be a text waiting for her. Maybe Holly had decided to visit her sister again. She had done it before.

Rebecca knew she was reaching. Holly always came home when she had class the next day. She worked so hard to keep her grades up at the small liberal arts college she attended—she wouldn't risk that to go visit her party-all-night sister. Except, sometimes Laurie hit rock bottom and pleaded with Holly until she felt guilty and went over. So there was a small chance. A very small chance, but it was the only hope Rebecca had to hold on to.

She hit the button on her phone and her heart thudded in her chest. One notification. She pressed the text icon. It was from Miles, sent late last night. Any warmth she might have felt that he had checked on her was drowned out by the knowledge that Holly hadn't sent her a text. Holly always sent a text if she would be late. She knew how much Rebecca worried. Holly worried just as much about any situation where Rebecca might be in harm's way. And why shouldn't she? She'd been there. They both had. For days, they had sat together, shackled in the dark, locked in that same small room. Waiting, as terror fogged their minds while hunger gnawed at their bellies.

But Holly and Rebecca had survived. Not all of them had.

Jasmine Winters hadn't made it out in time. She'd been strangled, mere hours before the police had broken through the basement door. They had all wondered who would be next…

No!

Rebecca squeezed her eyes shut and clenched her fists as she pushed that memory out of her mind. The darkness that tried to ooze into her mind didn't belong there. Not anymore. She'd banished that years ago, when she'd testified. When she and the other girls had put away their captor.

The memory of the trial made her shiver more. Would she never forget the face of their tormentor? He had been on his way to prison, and still he had held such control over the women he had terrorized. And he had known it.

He had control over her still—was still the face in her nightmares. What should she do?

Miles! He would probably check to see if she had responded to his earlier text. And he was a police officer. He'd know what to do about Holly.

Unlocking her phone, she pulled up his text. Her fingers trembled as she tapped out a message of her own, explaining the situation. She curled her lip as the auto correct kicked in, messing up a word of her message. She erased the word and started again. Many people would have sent the text anyway, trusting that he would understand. But this was too important. Plus, if she was honest with herself, she knew that people expected mistakes in her English, both because she had been Amish, and because she was deaf. It never failed to gall her. She hit Send.

Then waited.

And worried.

She tried to sit back down on the couch, but couldn't stay still. She bounced back up on her feet. She felt icky. Glancing down at herself, she grimaced. Not only was she still wearing yesterday's clothes, but her skirt was torn and wrinkled. And what if Miles decided to stop by when he got her text? She couldn't be seen this way. Ignoring the part of her that questioned why it mattered how she looked, she showered and dressed in clean jeans and an oversized royal blue sweater.

She checked her phone again. Still no word from Miles.

It was almost seven. She sent him another text, just in case the first hadn't gone through, then dragged out the Crock-Pot and started making chili. After she had the meat, beans and spices simmering, she stepped back and smirked at herself. What had she been thinking? She'd made enough to feed her parents and five sisters and brothers, when it was just she and Holly who lived in the apartment.

Holly.

Immediately, her mind was back in the middle of the current nightmare.

She glanced at her phone. The light was blinking. Maybe it was Miles. She clicked on the message, and his face appeared. The intensity of his blue eyes caught her unawares. Her breath caught in her throat. Those piercing eyes set in his honest face had attracted her from the first time she'd seen him. If only…

But it was no use. A man like him, strong and decent, wouldn't be interested in someone damaged like herself. Some of the members of her own community had been disgusted by what had happened to her all those years ago, even though she hadn't been to blame.

Besides, after what she had gone through, after what she had seen, she needed security in her life. A policeman who put himself in danger every day, no matter how handsome he was or how great he signed, was not on her list of possible mates.

Forcing her mind to accept the reality of her situation, she read his text.

Be there at 7:40. Jackson coming, too.

It was seven fifteen now. The sun was just starting to come up. She had almost half an hour. She'd go crazy just sitting here. To give herself something to do, she set about cleaning her already spotless apartment.

The light in the hall flashed. Someone was at the door. It had to be Miles and Jackson. The cautiousness she'd learned as a teenager wouldn't let her open the door without checking the peephole. Two men dressed in dark blue uniforms stood in the hall. She recognized the LaMar Pond uniforms. Miles and Sergeant Jackson. With a sigh of relief, she swung open the door.

The relief drained out of her when she saw how they looked. The tension emanating from the two men crackled like a live wire. She instinctively stepped back from them. Keeping her distance, she searched for clues in Miles's expression as he entered the apartment. The morning sunlight streaming in from the windows emphasized his serious expression. The downward curve of his mouth. The set of his strong jaw. Both spoke of a man on a mission. And an unpleasant one at that. Something bad had happened.

Fear lay in a leaden ball in her stomach. *Please, Lord, let everything be all right.* Even as she prayed, though, she knew everything was not all right. Something had happened to Holly. What? Sweat slicked her palms. She was about to find out.

THREE

Her throat was dry. "We can talk in the kitchen."

Miles nodded, then turned to say something to Jackson. She was fairly certain he was relaying her message to the other officer. In the kitchen, she grabbed a bottle of water from the refrigerator, then held it up with a questioning look. Did they want one? Both officers shook their heads. Fine. She uncapped it and took a long swallow. It made her throat feel better, but nothing else felt any relief.

Her stomach hurt. Not sick hurt. Scared hurt. The way it always had as a child. The way it had when she'd been held against her will ten years ago.

She scraped back a chair at the table and sat down across from Miles.

"Can you understand okay if I switch to pidgin? That will make it easier to keep Jackson in the loop."

She nodded. Pidgin sign language used mostly

ASL signs, but put them in English word order. This way, the signer was able to speak and sign at the same time. Not optimal, but she could follow along.

"Rebecca, I got your text this morning. I drove by the parking lot of the restaurant Holly works at. Her car was in the lot. But she was nowhere to be found. The manager said that she had left after she'd finished her prep work for the morning shift. That was around ten thirty. She never came back in. When he saw her car this morning, he thought she must have had car trouble and had someone pick her up."

What? That was absurd. If she'd left her car, she would have let them know so it wouldn't get towed. How could they not have realized something was wrong?

But she knew she couldn't really blame the manager. Holly's behavior at times was a bit erratic. She had already lost two jobs in the past for being unreliable. Mostly because she'd drop everything if her sister needed her.

"Her car was in disarray. Like someone had been shuffling through her things. Would she have left a mess if she was trying to find something?"

Judging from the skepticism scrawled across his face and seeping into his signs, Miles didn't think so. And Rebecca agreed. Her heart sank.

"Holly would never leave her things cluttered or messy," Rebecca informed him. His mouth was moving as he told Jackson what she said. She continued, "Disorder of any kind bothered her. I sometimes tease her that if there was a fire she'd make her bed before leaving the building."

The joke had made people laugh before. Not anymore.

"I want you to look at this picture," Miles signed. "Is this the vehicle she would have driven to work yesterday?" He tapped the screen on his phone, then flipped it around so she could see the picture he brought up. It was a white Jeep. He swiped his finger across the screen. A second picture of the back of the vehicle. The familiar vanity license plate came into view.

She swallowed. Nodded. Any hope she'd entertained that there might have been some mistake disintegrated. Something caught her eye.

"Wait, what's that?" She pointed to a large blot of color on the side of the car. It was a dark smear. It hadn't been there the day before. It looked like paint. Or…

A wave of nausea hit her, causing her to sway. "Is that blood?"

Miles hesitated. But the answer was on his face even before he nodded.

Holly wasn't just missing—she was hurt. *Why, Lord? Hadn't she suffered enough?*

She pushed back from the table, stood and moved to the sink. She gripped the counter with both hands, so hard her fingers hurt. Her control was slipping. The trembling started in her insides and worked its way outward. The view out of the window above the sink blurred.

A warm hand settled on her shoulder. Miles's fresh scent washed over her a second later. Without thought, she turned and burrowed into Miles's shoulder, fighting back tears. He patted her awkwardly on the back.

What was she doing?

Stepping away, she wiped at her moist eyes. More to give herself a moment to regain control than because she was crying. As she wiped her sleeve across her eyes, she gathered up the courage to face him. The compassion she saw in his expression was almost her undoing. Almost. But she was made of stronger stuff.

"Sorry," she signed.

He shrugged. "Not a problem. It's a completely natural reaction. Here's what we need to do. I need to bring you into the station to ask—"

"But I've done nothing wrong!"

He raised his hands, made a calm-down motion. "I know. We just have some questions for you, and they should be answered at the station so that we can bring in a certified interpreter to make sure there's no confusion or misinterpretation."

What? she thought. "You sign. Your ASL is beautiful."

She watched, fascinated, as his ears turned bright red. It would have been cute in other circumstances. "Thanks. But it's the law. You need a certified interpreter. Unless you agree to accept me as the interpreter for now."

She sagged back against the counter. "Fine. I accept. I don't want to go to the police station. What do you need to know?"

Miles took his seat back at the table. Reluctantly, she moved to sit down again.

The conversation started very generally. Age, birthday, job. Then it got more specific. Where did Holly grow up? Who did she live with?

"How did you meet Holly?"

"We went to the same school for years. Holly was a year ahead of me."

Jackson said something to Miles, who interpreted, translating it into sign. "You grew up in Spartansburg, right?" She nodded. "You lived in different districts. How did you go to the same school?"

She cocked her head at the officer. "Holly is hard of hearing. We were both bused out of district so we could attend the deaf program."

"Have either of you had an issue with violent boyfriends, or threats? Anyone hold a grudge against either of you at work?" Miles again.

She paused. "No."

But what about before? Was it relevant?

He waved his hand, drawing her attention back to him.

"If there's something that might be related, we need to know."

She drew a large gulp of oxygen into her lungs. She hated talking about this, and hadn't for years. Not even to Jess. But now she had to. Because Holly was in trouble.

"Ten years ago, when I was fifteen, I went out with Holly and three other girls from her school. Ashley Kline, Brooke Cole and Jasmine Winters. Ashley and Jasmine were older and had just graduated. Ashley was driving her mother's van and pulled over to help some guy who seemed to have broken down on the side of the road."

Abruptly, she stood and moved away from the officers. Memories of that day pulled at her, dragging her under. So much bad had come from one simple act of charity—stopping to help a stranger. Miles slowly got to his feet.

"Maybe we should go to the station."

She shook her head. She could do this. "No, I'm fine. There was just one man. He looked innocent enough. But he wasn't. He hadn't broken down. He was high on drugs and had stolen the car. When we stopped, he pulled out a gun and forced his way into the van and drove us to his house. He kept us locked up in the basement for two days. Until we were found."

She stopped. The memories were hitting hard and fast now. Overwhelming her. She could feel the cement wall against her back, smell the damp moldy basement.

Miles approached her carefully, as if he expected her to bolt. "I'm sorry you went through that," he signed. "And I hate that I have to ask you to relive it, but—"

"I understand," she interrupted. "It's for Holly."

"The man who abducted you, do you remember his name?"

As if she could ever forget. "Terry Gleason."

"Terry as in Terrence?"

She shook her head. "Just plain Terry."

Miles turned his head. Sergeant Jackson must have asked something. Miles nodded and then returned his focus to her. "The other girls, did they know the man?"

"I think some of them might have known him. Jasmine seemed to. She was the oldest. Already eighteen. And possibly Ashley. I don't know about Brooke. But I don't know from where. I didn't really know the other girls. And none of them could sign. Only Holly."

"You said you were fifteen? Did you still go to school together?" Miles pressed his lips together. She could almost see the thoughts running through his mind.

"No. I was still Amish back then so I only went to school through eighth grade." Regret surfaced, but she pushed away the feeling. Now was not the time. "The deaf program was a small group of students in a public school with a teacher of the deaf. Most of us went to her for Language Arts. The rest of the day, we were in classes with hearing kids and interpreters. Jess, Holly and I were the only three girls in the program. Jess left soon after I did to go back to her home school. That's when Holly started to hang out with the older girls. I met her again a few years later. I was in the middle of my *Rumspringa*." She signed "running around," using the direct translation. That was the only sign for the word she knew.

"Whatever happened to the man who kidnapped you girls? Please tell me he went to jail."

She nodded. "He went to jail. So it probably wasn't him. I testified at the trial. My parents did not want me to. Law enforcement and trials are not something Amish people usually get involved with. But I couldn't not testify."

Miles nodded, sympathy deep in his eyes. "Did all five of you testify?"

The dark hole she kept closed in her mind started to open, letting a few images spill into her brain. She slammed it shut, but some things could never be unseen. "Not all of us. Jasmine was strangled the day we were rescued."

Miles paled. His jaw hardened. Jackson's lip curled and his nostrils flared.

"I had never seen such evil. He left the rest of us after he had killed her. The police came while he was gone. Two officers. He came in behind them and attacked them with a bat. After one fell, the other knocked him down and handcuffed him. I didn't learn until the trial that the other officer had died from a blow to the head."

The officers looked at each other. Some kind of communication went between them. Their expressions darkened.

Miles puffed out his cheeks. She thought he resembled a blond chipmunk. Then he let out the breath and her pulse fluttered. This was no cute little boy. The man who stood before her was all cop, and his eyes were fierce. She trembled at the way his gaze sharpened.

"I need to find out what happened to that man. And if he is still in jail. That was ten years ago, so there is a chance he's free now. Not a very good one, seeing as an officer and one of the girls died. But I'm not comfortable not knowing everything."

Miles asked a few more questions, making sure he had the names of the other girls spelled correctly, and that he had the dates written down both of when they were taken and when they were found. Then he closed his notebook. "Our focus now is finding Holly. We'll pull Holly's driver's license photo from the database. Send it around to see if anyone recognizes her."

"Wait." He raised a questioning eyebrow. "That picture is almost four years old. She's lost weight and changed her hair."

Darting back into Holly's room, she grabbed Holly's tablet and clicked on the photo app. She used her finger to scroll through the pictures until she found the one she wanted. Perfect. It was recent enough that it had Holly's new trendy haircut.

She rejoined Miles and Sergeant Jackson at the table and handed over the tablet.

Miles took the tablet and held it so Jackson could see it, too. "That's Holly," she signed, and pointed at the laughing girl. Miles smiled, but his eyes narrowed. He had something else on his mind.

A second later, he proved her right. He tapped a second picture. When it filled the screen, he pointed to the girl next to Holly and signed, "Who's this?"

"That's Ashley. It must have been taken a few years ago, because she and Holly don't hang out anymore. They had some kind of argument over a man they had both dated."

"Ashley—" he checked his notebook "—Kline? Holly's friend from high school?"

"Yes, that's right."

He handed the device to Sergeant Jackson, continuing to sign as he spoke so that Rebecca would know what he was saying.

"Do you recognize her? I know I have seen her face somewhere, but can't place it."

Sergeant Jackson took the tablet and studied the photo. A frown etched itself into his face as he considered the image.

"Yeah, I have seen her before. But I don't know where. We need to get the pictures to the station, have them compared to the database. Could you email these images to us? Or maybe we could take the tablet, in case there are better images?"

Miles's hands flew as he interpreted. When he finished, Rebecca nodded. "Will Holly get the tablet back?"

Miles exchanged glances with Jackson. "If it's at all possible, we'll return it," he signed. What he didn't add was that it all depended on if they found Holly alive. It was in their expressions. She shivered. *Please, let Holly be okay.*

"I'm going to send those pics in now, actually," Miles interjected. Jackson raised his eyebrow. "That way they can start looking for Holly, and run a search on Ashley. But we will still need to hold on to the device, just in case."

Rebecca took the tablet back and shared the selected images in a text with Miles.

He pulled out his phone and looked at the images. Then he fiddled with his phone some more. "Done. I sent them in." He put the phone back in his pocket.

His watch lit up. She started. She recognized it as one of those new high-tech watches. It was neon green. Funny. She didn't often see people her age wearing watches. Watching his blond hair flop on his forehead, she decided it fit him.

"Lieutenant Tucker says he got the pictures and will make sure they are processed." His watch lit up again. He tapped it and read the message. "He also says that the visual artist can be there later this morning. You can come in and give her a description of your attacker. Maybe you'll remember something that will help us find him. We should head out. Jackson?"

The other officer nodded once, then got to his feet to head to the door. Miles stood as well, but instead of walking away, he moved toward her. He leaned forward, so close she caught the clean, sharp scent of him. No cologne, just soap, shampoo and Miles. "I can tell you this. I find it doubtful that you and your roommate would be attacked the same night by accident. Someone is after you. We just have to figure out who."

It took some doing, but Miles was finally able to convince Rebecca to come to the police station with him to give a description to the visual artist. It wasn't that she didn't want to help. Turning to the police just seemed to be awkward for her. Growing up, her community didn't go for outside help easily. He understood that. Even though she'd left the Amish community, she was still very close with her family. Those influences would be hard for her to overcome.

He also had a sneaking suspicion that her experiences with the legal system at the age of fifteen didn't help. He knew from watching the trial after his stepsister was murdered that people could be brutal to innocents. Especially the press.

He remembered the agony his father had gone through after his mother had been killed in such a sensational manner. He'd only been four, but some memories stayed with you forever. He shuddered as he remembered the way his father had been hounded by reporters, who wanted to know more about the famous model who'd died in a car crash while running off with another man. Leaving her child behind.

His father had become a broken man. But he'd had the wisdom to send his only child to live with his parents and younger brother. Spending the next two years with his father's deaf relatives had sheltered him from the worst of the drama, and connected him to a community he wouldn't have learned about otherwise.

"Hey, catch you later." Jackson sketched a casual wave and sauntered to his own car. Miles jerked back, grateful to be pulled out of his morbid memories.

"See you." Miles opened the passenger-side door for Rebecca, then jogged around to his own side.

As soon as the door shut, she turned to face him.

"Do you really think someone kidnapped Holly?"

How to answer that? Miles wasn't into giving false hope, but he also didn't want to escalate the situation with unsubstantiated theories. "I think we need to consider all the possibilities." There. How was that for diplomacy?

She wrinkled her nose. "But if it was the same person, why wasn't I kidnapped when that man attacked me last night?"

He twisted his body so he could give her his full attention. "I don't want to scare you. But we have no idea what your attacker would have done if you had not escaped. He may have meant to knock you unconscious and then kidnap you all along." She raised her hands, and he motioned for her to wait. "I don't have the answers yet. I intend to get them. Please, can you trust me a little longer?"

She didn't like it. He could see that, but she relented and let him start the car.

Twenty-five minutes later, he pulled into the station. As he led her into the building, he could see her shoulders stiffen. Her arms were folded in typical closed-off body language. He wished she would look at him, just so that he could send her a comforting look, or try to make small talk. Anything to make the situation easier. But she wouldn't look anywhere but straight ahead.

In the conference room, he saw that the interpreter had already arrived. Miles introduced the two women. Rebecca stared at the brunette with the edgy haircut with something akin to suspicion.

"Olsen!"

Lieutenant Jace Tucker approached, his forehead heavily creased. Uh-oh. Whatever happened, Miles wasn't sure he wanted to know about it. Jace Tucker was known for his no-nonsense attitude. He was also fair-minded. A man who commanded respect. Most of all, he was good at remaining calm and impartial, rarely letting his emotions show while he was working. That he looked visibly upset right now was a very bad sign.

"Yes, sir?"

"Is Miss Miller in there?"

What was this about? "Yes. I just brought her in to meet with the visual artist. She hasn't arrived yet."

Lieutenant Tucker craned his neck toward the room where he'd left the two women. Miles followed his gaze. The women were sitting quietly. Rebecca was staring straight at them. The lieutenant motioned for Miles to follow him. Instincts in high alert, Miles walked with him. They went into Lieutenant Tucker's office and shut the door. It took some effort, but Miles stood at attention, waiting for the other man to begin.

"We might have a witness to the attack on Holly," Lieutenant Tucker began.

Every muscle in Miles's body tightened.

"One of the tenants in the apartment across the street saw a man approach her as she was getting in her car. She couldn't see his face. He was wearing a mask. But she was able to clearly see that he grabbed the young woman.

She struggled, then sagged. He carried her to a van and drove off."

"Did she get a make? Model? Plate number?" The questions burst out of him. He couldn't have stopped them if he tried. Granted, he didn't try.

Lieutenant Tucker shook his head, the regret stamped across his somber face. "Sorry, Olsen. I wish she had. She had just taken out her contacts, and everything was blurry. The only reason she recognized Holly was because she went into the restaurant often and was familiar with all the employees."

He kept a lid on his disappointment. It was more information than they'd had five minutes ago. "So, on the positive side, we know two things. She was abducted and didn't leave under her own power. And, more importantly, we know she may be alive."

"Third," Lieutenant Tucker added, "it solidifies our suspicion that Miss Miller was attacked by the same person, given that the two women were both attacked by a man wearing a dark ski mask. And there's more."

How much more could Rebecca take? His gut tightened as Tucker gave him the rest of the news.

"How much can I tell Rebecca?"

The lieutenant hesitated. "I think we should go ahead and tell her everything. She needs to understand that this is a focused attack so she can stay vigilant."

Miles agreed, though he so didn't want to be the one to tell her and see that lovely face fill with fear. But, the flip side of that was he didn't want her to get the information through an interpreter, whose code of ethics stated she was there only to relay information. That would be such a cold way to learn such hard news.

No, he'd better tell her himself. And he needed to do it now. Waiting wouldn't make the news any easier.

Nodding to the lieutenant, he left the office and made his way back to the conference room. To his surprise, the other officer followed him. Taking in a deep breath outside the door, he hardened his resolve and opened the door.

And found himself looking straight into Rebecca's face. He and Lieutenant Tucker moved into the room. The lieutenant sat at the table. Miles moved to stand next to Rebecca. He nodded briefly at Tara, the visual artist, who'd arrived while he was talking with the lieutenant. Then he moved his gaze back to Rebecca.

Her gaze narrowed as she searched his face. He tried to school his features into a blank expression.

"What happened?" she signed.

He needed to work on his cop face.

"I will sign for myself," he informed the interpreter. "But I would appreciate it if you would voice what I sign for the benefit of the other people in the room." That way he could turn off his voice and switch totally to ASL instead of the pidgin he was using before.

Without displaying a flicker of surprise, she folded her hands into her lap.

"I was just informed we might have a break in the case," he signed, then went on to relate the first part of his conversation with Lieutenant Tucker—the information about the witness—to her. The only sound in the room was the low voice of the interpreter.

"So, she might be alive."

"I'm not going to say yes. I am going to say that I'm almost convinced my original thought was correct. I think your attacker meant to abduct you, as well."

"I concur," Lieutenant Tucker agreed after the interpreter finished voicing Miles's words.

Miles wasn't done. There was no way to soften it. Better to just tell her outright. Sucking in a breath, he prepared to deliver the devastating blow. He then told her the rest of what he and the lieutenant had discussed. "You remember the pictures you sent me? Holly and Ashley? I told you that I recognized Ashley."

Dread shifted into her face. She squirmed

slightly in her seat. He thought she looked like she was getting ready to run. Unfortunately, there was no escape from this nightmare.

"We found a match for her in the database. Two weeks ago, a woman matching Ashley's description was found unconscious in Cleveland. She'd been stabbed. The assumption is that either her attacker was interrupted, or he thought she was dead when he abandoned her."

Rebecca swallowed hard. Her lips trembled. She bit them. "Was her attacker the same person? The person who took Holly? And attacked me?"

She looked so forlorn. Tears were tracking down Rebecca's pale cheeks. Otherwise, her slim body was still. Shocked. He wanted to comfort her. But there was nothing he could do for her. Nothing except find whomever was responsible and put him away.

"It's possible, but there's a lot we don't know. We don't even know where exactly she was attacked. The police believe she was moved from the original scene. Until now, they had nothing to go on. No one had reported her missing. I have ordered additional precautions at the hospital, just in case her attacker gets the dumb idea to go after her again. Hopefully, she'll regain consciousness and be able to give us more to go on."

Suddenly, she gasped. "Brooke! Is she safe?"

"I intend to find out. And I will let you know."

"Why? Why is this happening?"

"I don't know yet. But I promise you, I will not give up until you are safe and the man responsible for terrorizing you and your friends is in jail."

FOUR

She wasn't happy.

She was scared, mad and moody. And feeling guilty, as she wondered if her escaping from her assailant had led to Holly being abducted. Then she'd remember that Ashley had been attacked, too. So maybe it was all a matter of time before they were each targeted, one by one.

She sat quietly as the car wove smoothly through the winding roads of LaMar Pond back to her apartment. Inside, though, she was anything but quiet. Inside she was a chaotic mess of whirling thoughts. Fear for herself, and for Holly and Brooke, filled her. Miles had already left a message with Brooke's family to contact him immediately.

The one positive thought was that she didn't have to go in to work today—she had already been scheduled to have the day off. Not that she would have gone. It would have been more than she could have borne to have gone back into the bookstore today, knowing that just yesterday someone had sat in her car, waiting to pounce on her. Someone who knew who she was and where she worked. Goose bumps broke out all over her. Tomorrow would be soon enough to face that fear. For now, she had to concentrate on going back to her apartment, knowing Holly wouldn't be there.

She shivered.

The car stopped. Looking up in surprise, she saw they had arrived. She had been so lost in her own mind, she hadn't even noticed how close they were.

Out of the corner of her eye, she watched Miles reach out and shut off the car before removing the key from the ignition. Every movement was quick and decisive.

"Let's go," he signed.

Ready or not, she mentally signed. *Not*. Sighing, she opened her door and followed him to her apartment building. She entered the security code, then they moved inside. They passed Mr. Wilson and his wife on their way up the stairs. The elderly couple moved slowly. Painfully.

All thought of her neighbors fled her mind as they approached her apartment door. The sudden, irrational hope that Holly might have found a way to escape and make her way home sprung up, only to die when she unlocked the door and entered the empty apartment. Holly's coat was not hanging on the hook, nor were her shoes on the mat beside the door.

But…

She shivered.

"Something feels off," she signed to Miles.

He frowned, but didn't mock her, or tell her she was imagining things. Instead, he motioned for her to stand against the wall while he drew out his gun. It still seemed odd to be around someone holding a loaded gun, knowing that he was willing to shoot or stand in front of her to protect her. The Amish didn't believe in violence. While her father and brothers would gladly put themselves at risk for her, she knew they would never consider shooting another person. Even if they or their loved ones were in danger.

But Miles was clearly prepared to do that.

She tracked him as he moved down the hall to the back of the apartment. He turned at Holly's room, sliding along the wall.

A movement broke her focus away from Miles. The closet door beside her was opening. Slowly, slowly. Like a horror movie. A sense of horrible fascination held her captive. She watched, dread building up inside her like a wave about to crest. When a large figure dressed in black slipped out of the closet, she broke from her haze. The figure halted, then charged at her, grabbing her in a viselike grip. His muscular hands squeezed her upper arms until they hurt and attempted to drag her toward the door.

A scream ripped from her throat.

Miles tore around the corner, his gun ready. The man jumped in surprise. He literally threw Rebecca at the policeman. Off balance, she sailed across the room, falling as she did so. Strong arms caught her, then let her go. Miles jumped past her and took off out of the apartment, following after her would-be kidnapper. She ran to the door and followed him down the stairs.

In the parking lot, Miles raised his gun again. He didn't fire.

The assailant barreled into frail Mrs. Wilson and knocked her to the ground. Agony spread across her wrinkled face. She wouldn't be getting up on her own power. Mr. Wilson sank to his knees beside his injured wife, his face pale.

The attacker never looked back. He hopped into a van that was idling. Into the passenger seat. An instant later, the van took off.

He had an accomplice. There were at least two people who they needed to track down before she could be safe again. Unfortunately, from where she was standing all she could tell about the other person was that he or she was wearing a baseball cap. The grimness that settled over Miles's countenance as his gaze met her eyes made her take a step back.

Miles shoved his gun back into his holster and jogged over to the couple, his hand already at the radio attached to his shoulder. Rebecca didn't need him to sign to know he was calling the 911 dispatcher.

The old man looked up angrily as Miles kneeled down beside the couple. He pointed a harsh, trembling finger in her direction. Uh-oh. She didn't know why, but the man clearly held her responsible for whatever had happened to his wife.

Miles shook his head firmly. He said something to the man. Both his expression and his body language indicated that he had spoken firmly, but not angrily. Like a man in command. The old man scowled, but backed down. Although his glance cut to where Rebecca stood. Even from a distance, she could sense the animosity simmering beneath his skin.

Before long, the ambulance crew and additional police arrived. The woman was put on a stretcher, then both she and her husband were off to the hospital. Rebecca recognized Lieutenant Dan Willis, brother-in-law to Jess's husband, when he hopped in his cruiser and followed the ambulance. No doubt to question the couple about the man who had barreled into them while he fled the scene. The man in the ski mask.

Rebecca waited in the parking lot with another officer while Miles and Jackson went over her apartment again, especially her closet. This time, they were looking for evidence of the man who had hidden inside, awaiting her return.

When Miles returned, she knew they hadn't found much.

"He was waiting for me, wasn't he?" she signed at him. "I don't think he knew you were there. I think he heard someone going back to the bedrooms, and thought it was me."

The smile Miles threw at her almost shocked her. What was there to smile about?

No. She took that back. She had a lot to smile about. *Thank You, Lord, that we are both safe. And please heal Mrs. Wilson.*

"I'm smiling because you're thinking like a cop," Miles signed back, his smile stretching into an infectious grin. Then it winked out. "But you are probably correct. I wasn't speaking, so he wouldn't have heard my voice. And I doubt he would have tried to grab you if he knew I was there. He risked not getting away in time."

She nodded. That's what she had thought.

"So why was Mr. Wilson angry with me? I didn't hurt his wife."

Miles blew out his cheeks and rubbed the back of his neck. Whatever it was, he didn't want to say. But she knew Miles well enough to know that he wouldn't lie. He would respect her right to know.

She braced herself.

Her skin was so pale, making her blue eyes appear huge. He was reluctant to add any more trouble onto her already overloaded shoulders. But keeping her in the dark would be unfair. It would be taking advantage of the fact that she couldn't hear the rantings of Mr. Wilson. It would be treating her differently just because she was deaf.

He hadn't grown up with deaf grandparents and a deaf uncle for nothing. He understood enough about deaf culture to know that one of the worst insults he could give this sweet, strong woman would be to judge her less than capable because she couldn't hear. His grandmother always told him that the poor communication between the deaf and hearing worlds often led to hearing people underestimating those who were deaf.

He bit the bullet.

"He said it was because of you that his wife was hurt," he signed.

She interrupted before he could go on. "My fault? But how? That's ridiculous."

He shook his head. "I agree. But there's a new development. Apparently, Holly's sister has been posting on Facebook about her sister's abduction. She mentioned you, and that the two of you were kidnapped before. A reporter approached them this morning. About an hour ago. He saw the post and thought it made a great story. Who knows who else has seen it."

Shock flared on her face, had her eyes shooting sparks. If he hadn't known she wasn't mad at him, he might've been tempted to take a step back.

"But how am I to blame? Or any of us. We were the *victims*!"

This was the pits. "I know, I know. But he was angry. His wife had recently had her hip replaced, and now she's hurt again. Angry people tend to lash out."

He was angry himself, right now. Not at the Wilsons, but at the man who had harmed the Wilsons *and* Rebecca, and who had also violated what should have been a safe space for Rebecca. He needed to do something. The feeling that he was going to explode worsened every time he imagined what could have happened to her if he hadn't been there.

But you were there. No sense dwelling on what could have happened.

It was a relief to see the other policeman come out of the building and give him a thumbs-up. She could go back inside. And stay there, alone? Uh-uh. Glancing up at the window of her apartment, he made a decision. Really, the decision had been made the moment that dude had tried to grab her.

"Come on. You can't stay here by yourself."

He waited for her to argue. She didn't. Instead, she lifted her shoulders in a listless shrug. "What are my options?"

"I think an officer should stay here with you. I can stay until this evening. I have my laptop in my car, so I can work from there. And then another officer can replace me. Sergeant Zerosky would be ideal. She goes on duty at eight."

The tension that had started to creep back into her posture bled out when she realized the officer staying overnight would be a woman. Hey, whatever made the intrusion into her life easier was fine with him. It made his job easier, too.

And he could go home and sleep. Not that he imagined he'd be sleeping all that well.

The idea of leaving her here, even with a decorated officer like Sergeant Zee, as they called the tall red-haired officer, left a bitter taste in his mouth. He really didn't like the thought of not being there. But he still had a job to do. And he would be back first thing in the morning.

It didn't help.

He spent the afternoon sitting on the couch, looking up leads on his computer. Rebecca was a very peaceful person to be around. She was a restful companion. Every once in a while, he'd glance over at her to see her reading a textbook or making notes.

Curious, he waved at her.

"Are you studying to earn a CDI certificate?" he signed when she finally looked up.

She nodded. "Yes. I have been working on it for the past two years. I have a bachelor's degree, which is required. I also have all my hours in. I need to take the first part of the test next month."

"Can I ask what inspired that?" It was an admirable goal, but not an easy one.

She grimaced. "The trial. The interpreter they had was wonderful, but there were some concepts that she still had trouble conveying so that I could understand. If she'd been able to work with a deaf interpreter, I think that whatever she'd signed could have been better translated through a person who knew exactly how a deaf mind works."

Wow, did that sound familiar. "My grandmother says the same thing."

Rebecca stood and stretched. The sunlight streaming through the window caught fire in her gold hair. Man, she was pretty. And honest. He had a feeling if she gave her word, she'd bend over backward to keep it. Unlike his mother.

Why had he gone there? His mother had nothing to do with the current situation.

"I'm thirsty. Want anything?" she signed, completely unaware of the dark place he'd gone to in his mind.

He shook it off. "Yeah, I could go for something to drink. What do you have?"

Please say Mountain Dew.

"Coffee, tea, water, lemonade. What's that face for?"

Had he made a face? Oops. He needed to be on guard more. This lady was an expert at reading the nonverbal signals most people were oblivious to. "Sorry. I was hoping you had some kind of soda." When her eyebrows rose to meet her bangs, he grinned and shrugged. "Actually, I really was hoping you kept Mountain Dew."

That cute little nose wrinkled. "No, sorry. I don't drink pop." She turned her left fist upright and smacked her right open hand on top of it in the sign for pop. The sound was strikingly loud in the otherwise silent environment.

He settled for lemonade, and then resumed working.

Twenty minutes later, he got her attention again. "I just received confirmation that Terry Gleason died in prison. So he's not personally responsible for any of this."

Abruptly, she stood, knocking her textbook onto the floor. She ignored it. He doubted if she even realized she had dropped it. She crossed her arms across her chest and rubbed her hands up and down her arms. Walked to the window. Came back. She continued pacing the room like a caged tiger for a minute or two.

He let her pace, recognizing the need to move while she digested the new information.

After a couple of minutes, she seemed to calm down a notch, although she still appeared disturbed. She didn't try to talk to him. Instead, she walked to the flat-screen television and swiped the remote control off the shelf. With a quick jab, she turned on the TV. The local news filled the screen. Huh. He hadn't realized it was already six in the evening. Closed captioning scrolled across the bottom of the screen.

The first story was a burglary in Erie. He grunted and nodded when the anchorwoman related that the suspect was in custody. Good.

The second story began. He sat up straight, his eyes flaring wide. Rebecca gasped and sank down into her seat. A picture of Terry Gleason filled the screen. Next were two side-by-side images of Holly and Ashley. Then a picture of Jasmine Winters. It was her senior picture, probably from the yearbook. A picture of Rebecca was last. Only Brooke's picture was missing. Did they not know about her yet?

Miles was barely aware of the story. All he knew was that their timeline had just moved up. Whoever was after these women had been moving relatively slowly, seeing how Ashley had been kidnapped weeks ago. Now, however, the perp knew that they were onto him, and had made the connection between the victims. A connection that would hopefully lead them to the identity of the attacker. Or attackers, since the man in the apartment earlier had clearly had an accomplice driving his getaway van.

Would the publicity and public scrutiny stop his vendetta? Or would this new development cause his attacks to escalate and become even more violent?

A hollow sensation took hold of his gut. The level of danger to Rebecca had just increased.

Miles immediately called in for more backup to watch over Ashley in the hospital. He'd also make sure Rebecca was never without protection. And he needed to find Brooke.

Things were going to get messy.

FIVE

Miles knew the news wasn't good the moment he walked into the station the next day. Lieutenant Tucker was waiting for him at his desk.

"What's up, Lieutenant?" He hoped with all his might that his instincts were off. But he knew, just from the troubled expression on the senior officer's face, that his gut was spot on. Something bad had happened. Real bad.

"A body was found early this morning. It had been dumped in the pond. Some fishermen found it. It was Holly."

Oh, man. He closed his eyes briefly. Poor girl. And poor Rebecca. He had to be the one to tell her.

"You sure, Lieutenant?" Of course Tucker was sure. Miles was grasping at straws.

"Yeah, I'm sure. The ME has already confirmed it and called her parents. It was her. She'd been beaten pretty badly before she was dumped in the pond. My guess is the perp kidnapped her so that he could take his time."

It made sense. The timing of disposing of her made sense, too—in a sick sort of way. "I think that news report last night might have been the reason she was killed now, rather than him running the risk of keeping her alive longer."

Lieutenant Tucker's eyes tightened. "I'm inclined to agree with you. I called Sergeant Zee. She's bringing Miss Miller in to give a full description of the man from the apartment yesterday. To see if there were any distinguishable marks on the man. Or on the vehicle. Anything to shed some light on this."

Miles nodded. "What about the couple who he ran into? They had said a reporter questioned them about Rebecca. Was it really a reporter?"

"It was. We confirmed that this morning. The reporter, however, had gotten an anonymous tip. Someone's been talking."

Great.

"What about the last girl? Brooke?" Tucker asked.

"I finally got a hold of her parents this morning. She's out of the country on a mission trip. They will call if anything suspicious happens."

Tucker nodded. "Very well. I'm going to go make some calls. I especially want to know what on earth made Holly's sister post about the kidnappings on social media."

Not long after, Sergeant Zee arrived with Rebecca, and escorted her into an interview room. Miles made his way back to Rebecca reluctantly. The last thing he wanted to do was to give her the bad news. But there wasn't any choice. Either she found out from him, or she found out from someone else. And he couldn't bear the thought of her having to hear the tragic news from someone she didn't know.

He'd wasted enough time. If he was going to protect her, he needed to get moving.

Setting his jaw, he shoved open the door and entered the room. Rebecca's head shot up, her blue eyes searching his face. The fear he saw there just about broke his heart before he pushed the emotion away. He couldn't let himself get distracted. Not now, when there was so much at stake.

He sat at the table across from Rebecca. The move was deliberate. He needed distance between them. The interpreter smoothly stood and moved beside him. He didn't even spare her a glance. Lieutenant Tucker shut the door and sat at the head of the table. He gave Miles a nod to go ahead.

Taking a deep breath, he began. "I have bad

news. Holly's dead. She was murdered early this morning."

All the blood leeched from her face. Tears pooled in her blue eyes.

He hated this.

"She was killed after the news reported her missing," she signed, her hands shaking. "And reported her connection to Terry Gleason."

He knew she'd pick up on that fact. "Yes. We believe the man is in a hurry to finish his attacks before he can get caught now that a connection has been made."

"Why wasn't Brooke's name mentioned?"

Lieutenant Tucker broke in. "Probably because she was a minor when it happened. I talked with Holly's sister this morning. She started this by posting about it on social media. But she never had Brooke's name. Even during the trial, Laurie wasn't there, and the names of the minors involved were not released."

Now for the new plan. Miles took over when the lieutenant stopped talking. "You can relax about Brooke. She's safe." For the moment. He quickly relayed what he'd learned that morning. "I don't think you should stay at your apartment tonight. It's just not safe."

She cocked her head at him, her brow crinkling. "But I thought I would have Claire with me again."

Claire? Oh! Sergeant Zee. He almost chuckled. There was so much innocence in her, even after all she had been through. She never tried to keep people at arm's length. Everyone was a friend. The amusement faded. As much as he hated the thought, it would be better for her if she stopped trusting so easily.

"Your apartment is too well-known now. Obviously, your attacker is aware of it. And the security code wasn't enough to keep him out. I don't think the place is secure. You'll be safer somewhere else altogether."

"Where will I go?"

"We'll think of that. First, let's go back to the apartment and you can pack a bag. Grab whatever you need to last you several days."

The moment the lieutenant gave him leave to go, they departed for her home. Jackson met them there. He waved at the other officer, who was on his phone. Jackson had come to add another layer of protection as Miles moved Rebecca. He followed her into the apartment and waited while she gathered her things. She came out of her room sooner than he expected.

"All done?"

"Almost. But I'm worried. My brother's getting married in less than a week. I can't miss his wedding."

Great. One more problem to work around.

Part of him considered telling her he couldn't guarantee that she'd be able to go. If her attacker was still at large, then even a special family event wasn't worth the risk. But looking at her weary face, he found he couldn't do it. He compromised.

"I can't make any promises, but if it's at all possible, I will get you to the wedding."

She wasn't completely satisfied with his answer, he could see that. But it was the best he could do under the circumstances. A frown pulled down the corners of her mouth. He had to give her credit, though. She dealt with her disappointment calmly and returned to her room to complete her packing.

He made a few phone calls while he waited. He had just ended a call when she returned, a large duffel bag slung over one shoulder. Her hair had been pulled up under a baseball cap. A backpack was on her back.

"Got your laptop? Your textbooks?"

She jerked a thumb at the backpack. "All in there."

He smothered a grin. She might not appreciate the sentiment, but she was adorable. And the image of the typical all-American girl. No one seeing her would have any clue that until a handful of years ago, she'd been part of the Amish community.

How difficult it must have been growing up unable to share more than the most basic communication with her family. It wasn't just that her family was Amish. He knew that many hearing families struggled learning how to communicate with their deaf children. But being Amish would have limited the opportunities and resources available to them. He was grateful that he could be there for her now, help her through this ordeal. Be her protector...

Mentally, he backpedaled. He was getting too involved. Too close to her. Experience had taught him that he made mistakes when his emotions were involved. Mistakes that had almost cost him his job. And could cost Rebecca her life.

He needed to distance himself. That was the only way he could keep her safe.

She was in the middle of a nightmare. Holly dead. Ashley in a coma. Who would be next? Her? Brooke? She was on the edge of a gigantic black hole, just waiting for it to suck her back into the vortex. Only this time, how would she get out?

Or would she be able to escape at all?

The last time had cost her so much. And not just the innocence stolen by the abuse the girls had endured. She'd been forced to make the decision that ultimately led to her leaving her Amish community. She didn't know if she had it in her to survive the terror a second time. Especially now that she was alone.

Alone. How was she going to be able to handle living in the apartment without Holly, knowing that her friend was never coming home? When Miles had decreed she couldn't stay there for the next few nights, she'd worried about where she would go—but she'd also been so relieved that she'd be able to get away. That she wouldn't have to stay somewhere where every corner reminded her of the friend she'd never see again. Where she couldn't block out the memory of her attacker grabbing hold of her, trying to drag her away.

Relief and confusion warred for her attention. She wanted nothing more than to follow blindly if it meant that she would not have to step foot back in that apartment. But that wouldn't be smart. She needed to be responsible. Which meant not letting Miles, as sweet as he was, make decisions for her.

Rebecca held her breath. If he suggested that the department would put her up in a hotel for the night, she would have to shut that idea down fast. That would put her way too far into debt. Not that they would ever expect her to pay them back. It was the principle behind the idea that mattered, though.

She shot a covert glance his way. He was standing, talking into his watch. She could see a piece of plastic in his ear. A Bluetooth. It seemed odd to her, but it fit him. He was obviously into gadgets. Miles shook his head. His bangs flopped across his forehead. My, he was adorable.

Which meant nothing, she reprimanded herself, ignoring the way her breathing hitched in her chest.

Sergeant Jackson entered the apartment as Miles finished his conversation and went to stand near him. Every now and then he would nod at something Miles said. A few minutes later, Jackson moved outside again and Miles made another call.

Rebecca hated to be petty, but the fact that she hadn't been in on the conversation really bothered her. Because she knew what they were discussing revolved around her. She and Holly and what had happened so long ago.

Don't be silly, she admonished herself. Even if she had been involved, she knew that it was also police business. Even if she had hearing, she wouldn't have been let in on those discussions. Anyway, she was used to being excluded from conversations. Growing up, neither of her parents had been able to become fluent signers. They had tried. She knew that. But Pennsylvania Dutch and ASL weren't exactly compatible. Her parents spoke English, it was true, but they always preferred their native tongue.

It wasn't all bad. Levi and Lizzy had learned ASL very well. Out of all her siblings, he and Lizzy were the ones she was closest too. At least emotionally. Thomas and Joseph were between her and Lizzy chronologically, but the boys had been too busy to learn more than rudimentary signs. The youngest, Ruth, had been just a toddler when she'd left the community.

"I have a plan," Miles announced, reverting back to ASL now that his phone call was done. "I was just on the phone with Jess. I'm going to drop you off at her house. She and Seth have agreed to let you stay with them. I've also cleared it for a cruiser to be placed on watch."

She shook her head. It wasn't that she didn't appreciate her friends, and the kindness of their gesture. She loved Jess, and Seth was great. But without warning, a deep longing for her mother filled the empty cavity in her chest.

"Can't I go stay with my family?" She put as much pleading into her facial expression as possible as she signed to him.

"Your family is Amish."

"I know that."

"We wouldn't be allowed to put a cruiser in front of their house. You'd be an open target. Especially with the renewed interest in the case."

"Would they even know that I grew up Amish?"

"I'm sorry." She believed him. Those deep blue eyes were pools of remorse. "I looked over the information from the trial yesterday while I was on my laptop. Your name wasn't released then, but the fact that one of the girls was Amish was. I can't take the chance. You'd be putting yourself, and your family, at risk."

He was right. As much as she wanted to argue, she had to accept it. She couldn't bear to bring this danger into her parents' home. Disappointment filled her. Lowering her eyes, she tried to conceal her feelings. A pair of spit-shined shoes entered her line of vision. Miles had moved to stand directly in front of her. She had to raise her eyes, tilting her head back so she could look into his face and see his hands moving.

"I wish I could let you go to your family. But you know it wouldn't be safe. At least at Jess's house, I can protect you."

And with that, she had to be satisfied. She followed Miles out to his car. Jackson was outside, standing guard. Rebecca turned and took one last look at her apartment building. Because there was no way she would ever be able to go back there now. She could return long enough to pack up her things for good, but she'd never live there again. Even while she had packed, goose bumps had popped out all over her skin. She had constantly looked over her shoulder. It was the quickest packing job ever as she threw her clothes in helter-skelter. She could only hope she had actually packed the clothes and toiletries needed to last several days.

One thing was certain. The moment this nightmare was over, she was looking for a new place to live. Even if she had to break her lease.

Within fifteen minutes, they were speeding on their way toward Jess and Seth's house. The darkness inside the car enveloped her like a cocoon. Her head started to nod. Leaning back against the headrest, she allowed herself to drift, thinking about the day's events.

A hand on her shoulder awakened her. Blinking, she pushed herself upright in her seat just as they passed the sign for River Road Stables. Jess had originally run the training and boarding stables with her brother, Cody. After he had died last year, she'd taken over the business. Seth and she now resided in the large white ranch house, which was adjacent to the stables.

The comforting scent of the recently mowed grass and dust mingled with the smell of horses drifted in through Miles's partially open window. She inhaled deeply, feeling soothed by the aromas that had surrounded her as a child in the Amish community. She tapped the button on her door panel to roll down her own window. A cool fall breeze tickled her cheeks, but she didn't mind.

The car swept past the stables and continued up the well-lit driveway. Jess had married a prince of a man. Seth had state-of-the-art security lights installed almost the minute they returned from their honeymoon. He knew how much his wife hated the dark—the result of a childhood trauma. The lights she'd had previously had been seriously outdated.

A pretty woman with a medium-brown ponytail moved onto the front porch as the car came to a halt. Jess. Rebecca hopped out of the car and ran up the steps to greet her friend. And to get into the familiar environment of the house.

She knew Miles was right behind her. She could feel his presence on the stairs behind her. His solid presence steadied her and brought her comfort. That worried her. She didn't want to start to depend too much on him. Yes, he could sign, and he was very protective. That didn't mean anything. He was a police officer. She was a case. That was all.

It had to be.

"Stay for dinner, Miles?" Jess signed and spoke simultaneously.

He flashed a brief smile, making Rebecca's pulse spike. "Thanks. But I need to get back to the station. Continue working the leads. I know Seth is working tonight, so you ladies lock the doors and set the alarm as soon as I go. A police car will be stationed here overnight. An officer should be here within the hour."

He waited for them to agree, then departed.

Rebecca watched his car turn around and start down the drive.

"You okay?" Jess signed.

Rebecca nodded her head.

"Okay. I left the phone in the kitchen. Seth wants me to call to let him know you arrived safely."

Touched, Rebecca hugged her friend. Pulling back, she signed, "Thank him for me, please. It really means a lot that you and he are letting me stay."

As she expected, Jess laughed and shook her head, making her ponytail bounce. "Silly. You're my oldest friend. Of course you can stay."

Rebecca watched Jess amble to the kitchen, taking all the cheer with her. Returning her gaze to the window, she sighed. Miles was gone. She hadn't expected him to stay. He had a job to do. And a killer to catch.

She had never felt so alone.

SIX

What kind of person kidnapped young women and murdered them?

Rebecca tried to study, but finally had to concede defeat. The events of the past couple of days weighed too heavily on her mind to allow her to concentrate on anything else. Setting her books and laptop aside, she went to her bag and pulled out her Bible.

Under the Bible was an old quilt her mother had made for her when she was younger. She pulled that out as well, then wrapped it securely around her shoulders. The blanket soothed her with the memories that were stitched into it. Martha Miller had made quilts for each of her children when they were young. A necessity when living in Pennsylvania where the winters were cold. She'd used the quilts as a way to teach her three daughters the fine art of quilting. Warmth mingled with disappointment in those moments.

Rebecca had sat at her mother's side, watching her hands carefully. She'd learned by watching how to form the stitches. Whatever words Martha had said, however, were wasted. She'd needed both hands for the sewing and could not use even the limited sign language she'd mastered to sign to her daughter. How could one feel so loved and so isolated at the same time?

She did, though. For most of her life.

Sighing, Rebecca turned to God for comfort, glad that she had really gotten to know Him through her friend Jess. Especially now, when she needed to be strong, and wasn't sure if she had enough courage to stand on her own.

Miles will protect you.

Would he? Had God sent Miles in His Providence? A protector who could communicate with her without needing to take the time to write everything down or go through an interpreter?

These questions were still swirling around in her mind when she went to bed an hour later. She had worried that she would be too wound up to sleep, but exhaustion soon caught up with her.

She woke up suddenly. Confusion and disorientation dazed her mind for a moment, until she remembered where she was. Jess's house.

The clock beside her bed said four thirteen.

She had hoped to be able to sleep in this morning. She sighed. It would have been great to snuggle back down under the covers, but she was wide-awake now. It would have been nice to talk with someone. No one else in the house would be up for at least an hour. If it was later, she could have used Jess's videophone to call someone. She'd used it to call the bookstore last night and talk with Tracy to let her know she might not be in today. Something she wouldn't have been able to do without the device. Tracy didn't sign. That wasn't an issue though. The videophone connected directly with the Pennsylvania Relay System. She'd been able to sign to the interpreter on her screen. The interpreter voiced what she signed to Tracy on the other end. It didn't even matter that Tracy was using a regular phone.

I wonder what Miles is doing?

She snorted. What did she think he was doing? Sleeping. The odds that he would answer a text or a call were not in her favor. Did he even own a videophone? He had to. Didn't he say once he had deaf grandparents? And the way he liked his gadgets, she couldn't see that not being one of them.

Antsy, she sat up and tapped the touch lamp near the bed once. The low light glowed like a night-light, making the room just light enough for her to see the shapes of the furniture throughout the room. Through a broken slat in the blinds, she could barely make out little pinpricks of light. She loved stars. They were like a connection to God. The window beckoned to her.

Turning the light off, she rose from the bed and made her way to the window. Easing herself down on the window seat, she rearranged and plumped the cushions behind her back before settling into the seat. Then she twisted the rod to open the blinds. The Pennsylvania night sky was awash with stars. They both filled her with awe and humbled her. She'd always loved watching the stars. She and her sister Lizzy used to crawl out their bedroom window and onto the back porch roof at night to watch the sky. They could sit there, silent, for hours. It had always been Lizzy she was with. Besides Levi, Lizzy was the best signer in the family.

Rebecca sighed, content for the moment.

But then all feelings of contentment disappeared. What was that light she saw? Something was flashing up in the trees. Or was there? Straining her eyes, she leaned forward, her nose almost touching the glass, trying to see if anything was up there.

Nothing.

She sat for another half hour, watching intently, arguing with herself about whether she had seen anything or was being paranoid.

What was she doing? Anyone looking toward the house might be able to see her with her nose pressed against the glass. Stumbling off the window seat, she hurriedly shut the blinds. Then she ran to the opposite side of the room.

Heart thumping, she stood in the dark, rubbing her hand over her heart as if she could slow it down.

What to do?

More cautious now that the possibility of a threat was there, she crept back to the window and moved the blinds slightly so she could look out. Nothing. Again. The only thing moving was the officer stationed outside the house. She'd forgotten about him. She must be losing her mind.

A few minutes later, the floor under her vibrated. The front door had slammed. She leaned closer to see that Jess was headed to the stables.

She tensed. If someone really was out there, would Jess be in danger?

Lights swept up the driveway. The morning help had arrived. She sighed in relief, sure that the threat was ended. The burly young man who exited his truck and followed Jess into the stables would surely deter anyone from coming any closer.

The moment Miles arrived, though, she'd make sure to tell him about her suspicions. No doubt, he'd search and find nothing. After all, who even knew she was here?

She just had to wait for Miles.

He couldn't sleep.

Flipping over onto his left side, Miles glared at the digital alarm clock as if it was to blame. Five after five. As in a.m. Unreal. It had been past eleven before he had managed to unwind enough to fall asleep. He was edgy about leaving Rebecca at Seth's, even with Thompson stationed right outside.

Why? It was secure. She was fine. He needed to stop worrying about her and get some sleep so he could find the lowlifes who had it in for her.

Flopping back onto his back, he resolutely closed his eyes. His alarm wasn't set to go off until seven. If he couldn't fall back asleep then he'd think about the situation. Images of Rebecca's face swam behind his closed lids. *Think of something else.* Mentally, he ran through the latest saxophone solo he had been working on.

Tossing and turning, he would doze off, only to wake suddenly. Minutes later, he was still thinking. He gave up. Throwing back the covers, he heaved himself to a sitting position. If he couldn't sleep, he might as well be productive. Hefting himself out of bed, he went through the motions of his morning routine.

He changed into his sweatpants and a police academy T-shirt. Then he got down to business. Stretching, sit-ups and push-ups got his blood pumping. Fully awake, he left his apartment for his morning run. Pacing himself, he kept his rhythm smooth. The sound of his feet hitting the pavement echoed in the air. While he ran, he allowed his thoughts to return back to the previous day.

Rebecca.

How was she holding up at Seth's house? Was she really safe there? He mentally squashed that worry as his foot hit a puddle and splashed water up his leg. Of course she was safe. Seth and Jess were both with her. They had installed a top-of-the-line alarm system after the attacks on Jess last spring. And he knew that Thompson took his duty very seriously.

Swerving around in the cul-de-sac at the end of the block, he began the return home. The sun was higher in the sky as he entered his apartment. He took a quick shower, changed and then grabbed a can of Mountain Dew and the pizza he had left over from the night before. He downed half the can while waiting for his breakfast to heat up in the microwave. Hearing it ding, he set the plate and the can on the counter and pulled his worn-out Bible off the shelf.

Best way to start the morning. Eating pizza and drinking Mountain Dew with Jesus.

Twenty-five minutes later, he set the plate in the dishwasher and made a basket into the recycle bin with the can. It clanked against the other cans. He'd have to empty that soon.

Now what?

His peace was interrupted as restlessness crawled through his bones. What he wanted to do was check on Rebecca, but he knew he couldn't. It was too early. And she was fine. *Stop worrying about her.*

Not happening.

He glanced at the clock. If he left now, it would be eight thirty when he arrived at the Travis home. Surely, that wasn't too early to stop by. She should be up. And if she wasn't, he knew Seth and Jess would be. Then he figured he'd get a head start on the business of the day. The sooner he found out who was targeting the sweet former Amish girl, the sooner she'd be safe. And off his mind.

Grabbing another Mountain Dew from the refrigerator, he bounded down the steps and out to his car, singing a song that he'd heard on the radio recently. He bopped his head to the music in his mind, causing his blond hair to flop on his forehead. Belatedly, he remembered that his neighbors might still be sleeping. A sheepish glance around showed the parking lot was empty, and there were no angry faces glaring out the windows. Shrugging his shoulders, he unlocked his door and slid into the driver's seat.

The drive was slow this morning. A thick layer of fog had fallen over LaMar Pond. Visibility was low. Taking his time, Miles bit back his frustration. It wasn't like he had to hurry to go to check on Rebecca. He had his pager on. And if there was an emergency, he would have heard the call come over the radio.

The emergency system had just hired a brand-new dispatcher. He hadn't met her yet, but she sounded young. Jackson thought she sounded pretty. But then, Jackson did like to flirt with the ladies. He never meant anything serious by it. Miles doubted he ever took any woman seriously. He frowned, as the image of Jackson flashing his charming smile at Rebecca hijacked his brain.

Maybe he should warn her about him. Make sure she knew the score.

Wait a minute. This wasn't any of his concern. And besides, Rebecca seemed far too reserved to put up with his jokester coworker.

And her roommate had just been murdered.

And she might be next.

All thoughts of Jackson fled as the reality of the situation again came to the forefront. Tightening his grip on the steering wheel and on his wayward thoughts, Miles maneuvered the sleek cruiser off the smooth paved road and onto the dirt back road that led to the stables. Immediately, the car bounced as his front tire hit a pothole in the road. It was more like a crater. He grimaced. Too many bumps like that and he'd do some real damage to the car. Just what he needed when he was trying to convince the chief that he was responsible.

Up ahead, he could make out the sign to River Road Stables. A surge of adrenaline caught him off guard. Straightening in his seat, his eyes shifted in every direction as he pulled up the driveway and looked for any signs of trouble. His tension didn't let up as he passed the lower barns. As he drove by the upper barn, he noticed the brand-new horse trailer parked out front. That wasn't worrying—in fact, it was probably good news. Business was doing better for Jess, now that her late brother had been cleared of all the charges that had been brought against him last year.

Miles headed up the lane to the house. His heartbeat quickened. He swung the car into the space behind Seth's pickup truck and stepped out of the car, waving at Thompson. The other man grinned and gave him a thumbs-up before heading out. That was fine. Miles didn't mind staying until the next shift arrived.

The hair on the back of his neck prickled. He swiveled his head around, eyes narrowed as he looked for threats. Nothing. But he couldn't rid himself of the feeling that someone was watching him.

His right hand settled on his revolver as he stepped away from the vehicle. The feeling of the gun was reassuring, but he quickened his pace as he strode up the walk.

A movement in the front window caught his attention. He turned his head. And forgot how to breathe.

Rebecca had pushed back the blue drapes and stood watching him, the lace sheer covering her but not hiding her. Like a wedding veil.

Whoa, buddy. Don't even go there.

He waved at her. She waved back and offered him a smile so radiant, it made his chest tight.

Then she whirled and vanished from sight.

Less than a minute later, he heard the click and twists of the locks and bolts being undone. The door swung open, and Rebecca stepped out to greet him. Her hair was pulled back in a French braid. Without the hair framing her face, her cheekbones seemed impossibly high and fine. Delicate.

Abruptly, he realized he was staring at her. His face heated as he lowered his head. His bangs flopped over his forehead. He brushed them aside as he brought his head back up... and his eyes caught on something glinting in the trees.

Fully alert, he motioned Rebecca back. Then he saw it, the muzzle of a gun. The picture window she'd stood in front of a minute before shattered. Without thinking about it, Miles jumped toward Rebecca, pushing her to the ground and covering her shaking body with his. A second slug hit the porch, sending wood chips flying in every direction.

Miles raised his head and looked at the damaged area. His blood froze.

If the gunman had been two seconds faster, Rebecca would be dead.

SEVEN

Miles shot to his feet, his hand pulling his gun from the holster in the same movement. A motor roaring to life beyond the trees caught his attention.

Whoever it was, they were getting away.

"Are you hurt?" he signed, checking her pale face for signs of pain. He saw fear and more than a little shock, but no injuries. As soon as she shook her head, some of the pressure in his chest eased up.

Stepping in front of Rebecca, he motioned for her to stay down. Just in case the car he had heard wasn't the shooter. *Or,* his mind whispered, *if there was more than one person up there.*

Seth burst into the hall. "Was that a gunshot? What's going on?"

"Get her in the house and stay away from the windows."

Miles risked a brief glance to see that his orders were being obeyed. They were. Rebecca had already been hustled into the house and out of his sight. Out of the sniper's sight, too.

Gun ready, Miles edged behind the column on the porch and peered toward the hillside. Nothing visible. Which meant absolutely nothing.

Not taking his eyes off the line of trees where the shots had come from, he used his left hand to find his radio and called for backup.

The wait for help to arrive seemed to last forever. In reality it was only about ten minutes. Lieutenant Jace Tucker was the first to arrive, followed shortly by Lieutenant Dan Willis and Jackson. He did a double take when he saw Jackson. Jackson wasn't on the clock until noon. Same time as him.

Being a cop, though, meant you were always prepared to answer a call.

"Shooter, up in the trees," he said to the men. "It appeared the shots were intended for Miss Miller."

Lieutenant Tucker nodded, his own blue eyes squinting toward the hillside. "How many shots, Olsen?"

"Two, Lieutenant. One hit the window, and the other the porch." He indicated the damaged area behind him. The other officers all whistled at the hole in the porch. Miles tried to hide a shudder as he recalled how close it had come to Rebecca. He was completely sure it was God's protection that had saved her. Saved them both.

"And Miss Miller?"

"She's fine. In the house with Seth."

"How do you want to play it?"

That gave him a start. Then he remembered. He was in charge of this case. The chief must have passed the word along.

"We need to sweep the trees for evidence. I doubt the shooter stuck around. I heard a motor revving up in that direction right after the shots were taken."

"You joining in the search?" Lieutenant Willis pulled his sunglasses down over his eyes. He suddenly looked every bit the former soldier that he was.

Miles hesitated. But only for a moment. The urge to stay with Rebecca was strong. But he didn't need to. Seth was present to interpret— he wasn't completely fluent but he was good enough to handle just about anything conversational. Moreover, Seth was a paramedic, and would make sure that Rebecca hadn't been injured. Yes, she'd be well taken care of inside— she didn't need him there. His place was with the team, to make sure the area was safe. That she was safe.

"Yeah, I'm coming. Jackson?"

"I'll remain on guard," Jackson responded.

Wow. He'd expected a bit of an attitude. Jackson was a sergeant. As Jackson joined him on the deck, he clapped a hand on Miles's shoulder.

"Don't worry, Olsen. I'll take care of your girl," Jackson said in a low voice before heading inside.

A leaden ball settled in Miles's gut. Apparently, he hadn't been able to hide his growing attraction to the former Amish girl.

No matter. He had a job to do.

The search didn't take long. Within the space of an hour, they had found the place where the shooter had hidden. It wasn't difficult to spot. Branches had been sawed off trees and left in a pile. From the resulting hole, Miles had a clear view of Seth's porch. How did the perp know that Rebecca would be here? She really didn't have time to tell anyone. Unless she had contacted her family after the fact so they wouldn't worry? Still, Miles had a hard time envisioning her family giving out information about her. She might have left the community, but they were still Amish and tended to keep to themselves. No. It had to have been something else. He'd kept a close eye on the rearview mirror the whole time they'd driven here the previous night and he was sure they hadn't been followed. So what had given her hiding place away?

What was that on the ground?

Miles kneeled down beside the tree. There, on the ground, was a small, pink blob with tooth marks in it. Of all the stupid, careless mistakes for a wannabe killer to make!

"Lieutenant Tucker!" Miles was careful not to touch the object or the area around it. "I have some evidence to bag."

Tucker trotted over and peered over Miles's shoulder. His exclamation made Miles smirk. "Of all the dumb things…is that chewing gum?"

"Yep. Sure is, Lieutenant. Freshly chewed and loaded with DNA."

"Oh, yuck." Dan Willis stopped by to check out the discovery. "Well, isn't that disgusting? But sure is a nifty clue."

"Yeah." Miles carefully bagged the evidence. "Who knows how long it will take to process, though. LaMar Pond is hardly like one of those shows on prime-time television. And when it comes to the district's crime labs, we always have to wait our turn."

Tucker grimaced. "Ask the chief if he could try to put a rush on it."

Miles nodded, although secretly he wondered what good that would do. There was only so much pull a small-town chief had, especially surrounded by bigger departments with higher crime rates.

"You know, even if the results come back and you find the chewer of that gum, that won't be enough to prove anything."

Miles ducked his head in acknowledgment of the fact.

"I know. This gum is just circumstantial evidence, but it is a place to start."

"That it is."

The officers completed processing the scene. Miles was antsy to get back to Rebecca. He needed to reassure himself that everything was well. He also needed to get into the office so he could continue hunting whomever it was who was attacking women and now had Rebecca in his sights.

Even though Ashley and Holly had not been shot, Miles was convinced Rebecca's attacker and the one who had attacked the other girls were one and the same. It would be too much of a coincidence otherwise. He needed to find the connection to the kidnapping ten years ago. Fast.

Rebecca was sitting in the kitchen with Jess when he returned to the house. A cup of tea was cradled between her hands, but he doubted if she was truly drinking it. It was more likely just a prop to keep her hands busy.

Miles grabbed the chair across from her and

pulled it next to her, angling it so that he could look directly into her face. Into those blue, blue eyes. He blinked, and refocused. "I'm sorry that you have to deal with all this. I will do my best to get you some answers as quickly as I can. I want to catch the person who is after you."

"I'm scared," she signed back. His heart ached at the sorrow he saw in her hunched shoulders. "Not just for me, but for Brooke. And Ashley."

Understandable.

Lieutenant Tucker and Jackson joined them. Jess rose and left them, telling Rebecca she'd be there if she needed her. Miles switched back to pidgin, interpreting for Rebecca with her consent.

"I was wondering about the night you were attacked in your car. You said that your boss had asked you to close for her. Is there any way anyone could have known this?"

She cast her gaze down to her folded hands for a moment. He wondered if she was going to answer when she looked up again. "I suppose it's possible. April had been planning to go out of town this weekend to see her parents. Her mother had asked her to go a day early. She asked me a week ago if I could take the closing shift alone."

Which meant anyone who talked to April could have gotten that information.

"Did closing by yourself bother you? Please don't take this the wrong way, but most customers can't sign."

A brief smile lit her face. "Most of the people are fine using paper and pen to talk with me. Besides, I was only alone an hour before the store closed. We don't usually have many customers at that hour anyway. Most of the work I did was closing out the drawer and getting things put away."

"Is April still at her parents' house?"

She nodded, and Miles made a note to himself to confirm it. That was easy enough to check out.

"Rebecca..." He paused, trying to figure out how to phrase the question. Then he decided to just put it out there. She wouldn't hesitate to ask the same question if their positions were reversed. "Did you tell anyone where you were staying last night? That we had moved you here?"

A blank look. Then slowly, like the dawn rising, he could see the comprehension and consternation moving into her face. He liked the way he could tell what she was feeling at a glance. No secret motives there. He doubted if she could pull off hiding her emotions.

"Yeah," she signed, bobbing her right hand

at the wrist like a nodding head, the thumb and pinky spread out while the other digits were folded over against her palm. "Tracy, the other girl who works at the bookstore. I'm supposed to work with her today. I told her there was an incident and that I was staying with a friend. I also told her that I'd call her later to let her know if I would be able to come into work today."

Miles's first instinct was to give her a resounding *no*. She couldn't go into work today. He wanted her to stay safe. But where was safe? She ought to have been safe at the Travis home. Now that her location was known, he'd have to see about extra patrols here.

And, he needed to check on some leads so he could solve this case.

But in the meantime, was it really that dangerous for her to go to work? If she was at the bookstore with an officer, she should be okay. Obviously, he would drive her to and from the store. As much as he wanted to stay with her, he had a job to do.

A red flag went up as he realized how much he wanted to stay with her. But he needed to be the one working the case. Chief Kennedy was counting on him. Even more than that, he was aware that he wouldn't rest easy unless he knew for sure every rock was being overturned to find the culprits. And that meant he was getting too close, too involved.

He needed to get this done so he could step away.

No good would come from entanglement. Hadn't his mother's betrayal and death taught him that? Even though his father had later re-married a wonderful woman, the betrayal of his first wife had led to the mistrust that had ulti-mately destroyed that second marriage. Miles wouldn't become the fool his dad had been. Even being alone was preferable to that.

The words sounded good. But the hollow pang in his heart mocked him.

She didn't like the way Miles's expression had darkened. His face was neutral enough, but the pain in his eyes overwhelmed her. She wanted to reach out and grab his hand, shake him out of his black thoughts. Offer him some of the comfort he had so generously given to her over the past few days.

Instead, she placed her hands firmly on her lap while she waited for him to speak. The effort to not interrupt his thoughts and argue that she should go to work turned her knuckles white. A quick burst of pain shot through her palms. When had she fisted her hands? Her finger-nails were digging in deep. *Mam* frowned on her longer nails. Her pretty pink painted nails. Nails that weren't practical at all, but fancy for no reason other than that she liked them that way. Right at the moment they were causing her more discomfort than they were worth. She intentionally unclenched her hands, stretching them wide.

"You okay?" Miles was looking at her, his brow wrinkled in concern.

He was just a tad too observant. It was useless to try and control her facial expressions. They were too ingrained in her, and were as natural as breathing.

"Fine," she signed back, tapping the thumb of her right hand into the center of her chest, keeping her fingers spread wide. "I just scratched myself with my fingernails."

He nodded, accepting her excuse.

No wonder. There were other things to consider.

"Here's my thoughts." They weren't happy thoughts, judging by the frown on his face. He switched back to pidgin. "I think you should go into work. I need to check out the leads we have. I will ask Chief Kennedy to have an officer meet us at the shop so you won't be alone."

Rebecca chided herself for the spurt of disappointment that his words evoked. Well, of course he couldn't stay with her. He had a job to do. It wasn't like she was anything more than his latest case. Anyway, it would be better for them to spend some time apart. She was far too attracted to him as it was.

"Let me call Tracy. Let her know I'm coming in later. What time? I work from ten to four every Saturday."

Miles brought his arm up to glance at the watch on it.

"It's ten thirty now. Tell her you'll be in before noon. I will drop you off before I go into work. That will give the chief time to find coverage to stay with you while you're there. Which means I should call him now. Excuse me."

Before she could respond, he turned and left the room, tapping on his watch and talking. Why did the room feel so empty without him? Weird. She really needed to stop staring at him. Especially since two of his colleagues were sitting at the table with her. Face burning, she tried to be nonchalant as she met their gazes. Fortunately, both men were professional in their demeanor.

Awkwardness set in. They couldn't speak with her, not with Miles out of the room, and they appeared to be unsure if it would be impolite to carry on a conversation that would exclude her. She had to appreciate the sensitivity. Many people would have been completely unaware of how left out and alone she felt while they conversed. Even her parents had not been aware of how abandoned she often felt, sitting alone in silence at mealtimes while the flow of conversation and activity moved around her. When her throat grew hot and tight and her eyes burned, she realized she had let her past take control. Again.

When, Lord? When will I learn to control my emotions? To let go of these feelings?

Tired of feeling useless and sorry for herself, she stalked to the stove. Nothing soothed her like cooking or painting did. Since she had left all her art supplies at the apartment, cooking was her best option. Jess hadn't started lunch yet, and Rebecca really needed to eat before she went into work. With all the excitement that morning, she had forgotten all about breakfast. But now she was remembering with a vengeance. Her stomach was starting to churn, as hunger rippled through her.

Bending down, she dragged a pot out of the cupboard and filled it with tap water. Water sloshed out of it as she set it on the burner. She felt the handle vibrating in her hand from the force with which she'd slammed it down. Wow. She hadn't meant to be so aggressive. She shrugged. No harm done.

Footsteps vibrated behind her. She whirled

around as Miles burst through the door. His gaze darted back and forth, searching for something. What was wrong with him? There was a wild glint in his eyes. Lieutenant Tucker and Sergeant Jackson both came half out of their seats, their hands flying to the guns strapped into their holsters.

"What's going on?" Miles demanded, his signs abrupt. "What crashed in here?"

Sergeant Jackson settled back in his seat and crossed his arms, a mocking grin on his face. He uncrossed his left arm long enough to jerk a thumb in her direction. Miles started to sign to her what he said, hesitated, then continued, flicking a concerned glance her way.

"Jackson says you were banging the pots around. Are you angry? I'm sure your boss would understand if you didn't go to work today given the circumstances."

Lieutenant Tucker rolled his eyes. Sergeant Jackson's smirk widened. What? She looked closer. Miles's ears were turning red. Apparently, that wasn't all Jackson had said. Her lips tightened.

"I want to go to work. And I was feeling frustrated by the situation. Which I think is normal."

He nodded and interpreted.

Her eyes narrowed, and she fixed a hard

stare on Sergeant Jackson while she continued to sign. "Please inform Sergeant Jackson that it is rude to say things in front of me that you would not feel comfortable interpreting."

Jackson's mouth dropped open, making him resemble a fish. A tide of red surged up his neck and face, melding with his hairline under his dark hair. Miles smirked and slapped him on the back. She could see Jackson's lip curling up in a mock snarl. Then he gave Miles a playful shove. And Miles shoved back. Within seconds, they were both grinning.

They were like children. Full-grown men with difficult jobs and important responsibilities…goofing off like children on a playground. Shaking her head, she turned around and grabbed up one of Jess's magazines to leaf through while she waited. After a few minutes, she switched her attention back to her pot of water, now boiling on the stove. She measured out two cups of macaroni. Stopped. Measured out two more. None of these men were small. They all were tall and muscular. And they had worked hard combing the woods. She shuddered, remembering why. No! She would not dwell on that. God was in control. She needed to give Him the fear. Still, her stomach turned and quaked. The fear in her was so strong, she knew it would choke her if she didn't control it. Forcing herself to concentrate on fixing the meal, she measured two more cups of macaroni, ignoring the way her hand shook.

Someone entered the room. She froze, then relaxed as another officer entered the room. It was Claire. Rebecca smiled at the red-headed officer who had stayed with her two nights earlier. The woman had so much responsibility on her plate, but seemed to be handling it well.

She tracked the young officer's path across the floor to the table where the men sat. They all looked up at her arrival. Their faces showed varied levels of expectation and dread. Why dread? With a grimace, the woman slapped a crinkled picture in the center of the table. Rebecca wrinkled her nose. She could see the mud stuck to the picture from where she sat.

Miles shot to his feet, jerking his head in her direction. Lieutenant Tucker said something to the woman, and she responded. Both faces were grim.

Rebecca clenched her jaw. Lipreading had never been her forte. As many times as she had insisted she didn't care, she wished she could just this once.

What was in that picture that had Miles so shook up?

Curiosity burned in her mind. Without making a deliberate decision to do so, she stepped toward the table to get a better look. And felt her world tilting.

Bile surged in her throat. She was choking. She couldn't breathe. The picture lay there, mocking her. The glass measuring cup slipped from her numb fingers, shattering on the immaculate kitchen floor. Macaroni and glass flew in every direction.

Footsteps. Miles was there, his big hands warm on her shoulders. Every other part of her was so cold. The panicky thought flitted through her mind that she'd never be warm again.

She could feel his gentle breath on her ear. She shivered. He was talking. She felt more footsteps. Police were on every side of her. And Jess was there, taking her arm. No doubt she'd heard the crash. Jess could hear quite a bit with her hearing aids in.

She shook off Jess. Her friend didn't understand. She hadn't seen it. She didn't know. Her arm weighed a ton as she pointed at the offending picture on the table. Miles's hands tightened on her shoulders before he turned her away from it and pulled her head against his chest, shielding her. She burrowed in, squeezing her eyes closed. She felt Jess grab her hand again. This time she didn't shake her off, but held on tight.

Raising eyes that burned, she caught sight of Jess's ashen complexion.

Feeling like her right arm was coated in cement, she raised it, signing to Jess and Miles, "That picture was in a frame on my desk. I didn't notice it was missing before. It was taken last year."

Jess rubbed Rebecca's cold hand briskly between her own two warm hands. The masculine arm around her shoulders tightened. But no matter how much they comforted her, she didn't think she'd ever rid herself of the image of her, Jess and Holly, laughing at the camera. Or the big red *X* slashed through Holly's face.

EIGHT

Rebecca pulled away from Miles. His arm moved from her shoulders, but he kept the palm of his hand firmly on one. The warmth sank in, sending a flow of comfort coursing through her. Lieutenant Tucker took his place on her left side. She allowed the two officers to lead her around the debris and back to the table. Miles let her go long enough to sweep the disturbing picture off the table and hand it to Jackson, who neatly shoved it inside his jacket.

Lieutenant Tucker left her side once she was situated. He said something to Jess, who gave a jerky nod before disappearing. A moment later, she came to the door of the kitchen and handed him a broom and dustpan.

Her eyes met Rebecca's. Years of friendship trickled through that glance, and Rebecca read her concern and fear in an instant. "I'm fine," she signed to her friend. "I have two cops right here with me."

Some of the worry left Jess's expression. But her face was still shadowed. "Okay. I'm not abandoning you. Jace has asked Seth and me to remain in the other part of the house while the police investigate this situation."

Jace? She was confused for a moment before a lightbulb switched on in her brain. Lieutenant Tucker. She couldn't bring herself to think of the man so casually. Although she did remember seeing him and his pretty wife at Jess's wedding.

The wedding. A happy time so far removed from all that was happening now.

Miles pulled a chair close to her and sank onto it, about a foot away from her. If she stretched out her hand…

Wait. What? Relying on a man was not something she wanted to do. But it was Miles, her mind argued. He was sweet. And protective. And she trusted him. Didn't she?

Without warning, another face shot into her mind. A smile that had seemed innocent at first. Only later did she see the menace behind it. Shackles on the wall stood in stark relief in her memory. She rubbed her wrists as if she could still feel them cutting into her skin. The total darkness of the room. The complete lack of sight and vision had preyed on her senses, on her emotions, for what felt like much longer than the two days until she was rescued.

A face appeared in her line of vision, and a hand tapped her arm. Instinctively she recoiled. Then regretted it as hurt flashed in the blue eyes before her.

When would she ever learn to control her reactions? Was she destined to live in fear of men because of one man's actions? Not all men were cruel. And not all touches were bad. Forcing her breathing to slow, she worked her mouth into what she hoped was an apologetic smile. "Sorry," she signed. "I'm freaked out right now. Didn't mean to react so much."

A streak of warmth returned to his face. "I understand."

Before he could continue, she broke in. The questions were fizzing up inside her like a bottle of soda that had been shaken. She could feel the pressure.

"Where did Claire get that picture?" She swiveled her head around. The female officer had taken off. As had Jackson.

Miles intercepted the next question. "Jackson and Sergeant Zerosky are headed back out to the station. The picture was found on the road near where we think the shooter parked his vehicle."

"Why would he need it? Was it to terrorize me more? To taunt me?" A single tear escaped and ran down her cheek. She swiped it off with her fist. Now was not the time to cry. She wanted answers. Correction—she wanted her life back. Now.

Miles let out a sigh. It was hard enough to ruffle the bangs on her forehead.

"It wouldn't make sense for him to taunt you. That doesn't seem to be his method." His signs paused. He tilted his head and tapped one long forefinger against his chin.

Rebecca sucked in a breath. Held it. He was debating how much to tell her. She didn't want him to clam up now. And too much of a reaction might convince him she could not handle the truth. Which, if she was honest with herself, she was not sure she could. But to be left in the dark was not something she was willing to accept.

It felt like forever as she waited. Finally, he seemed to come to a decision and raised his hands to resume signing. She let out her breath. "My best guess is that someone gave him the picture so that he would recognize his targets. The lieutenant agrees with me."

Rebecca raised her hands then dropped them again. There were just no words. She went numb. A helpless shrug was all she could muster to convey her complete sense of discombobulation.

"I will figure it out," Miles signed, an earnest

frown wrinkling his brow. His hair almost covered it. In normal circumstances it would have been adorable.

The need to escape was strong. Overpowering.

"I need to get ready for work."

Rebecca bolted from the room and raced down the hall. Diving into the guest room Jess had prepared for her, she shoved the door closed behind her. All at once, her burst of energy drained out of her. She felt shaky and weak. Leaning against the door, she pressed her forehead against the wood. As if the pressure could erase everything she'd been through in the past few days.

If only. She squeezed her eyes and lips tightly shut, straining to hold in the tears that wanted to break free, but they couldn't be repressed. Her levee was broken. Hot tears cascaded down her face. Turning from the door, she crashed down onto the bed and pulled the pillow to her. Held it to her mouth to bury whatever sound she made while weeping. She'd learned early on that hearing people could hear her when she sobbed. Muffling the sobs as best she could, she allowed herself the luxury of her tears. For herself. For Ashley. And especially for Holly.

Half an hour later, she presented herself to Miles, outwardly calm and ready to go to work.

If Miles noticed her red, puffy eyes, he was kind enough to ignore them.

When they arrived at the bookstore, he spent a few minutes questioning Tracy. Rebecca wasn't privy to the conversation, but judging by the way Miles tightened his lips, he wasn't happy with her answers.

He stalked over to Rebecca, blue eyes shooting sparks. "Sergeant Parker just pulled up. He will remain on the premises until your shift is done and then drive you back to the Travis's home. I am heading into the station, but I will call you tomorrow morning."

"Wait!" She pulled at his sleeve as he made to leave. "What did you ask Tracy? I could see that her answers annoyed you."

He shrugged, his lips twisting. *He's not going to tell me*, she thought.

"Please. I need to know. Do you think I will be safe here? Has she noticed something suspicious?"

Miles turned his blue eyes directly on her, and she felt her face warm. Inside her stomach, she had a fluttery, squirmy feeling. What was it about him that disturbed her equilibrium so bad? She had never felt this way around any man. In fact, since she'd been kidnapped, she avoided men. Feared them. She had learned firsthand what her mother had tried for years to instill in her. A handsome face sometimes hid an evil heart.

But Miles didn't inspire fear. She wasn't afraid that he would try to control her, to over-power her. Instead, she felt safe and protected when in his care.

Which probably wasn't good. It meant she was dropping her guard.

Lifting her gaze back to his face, she saw his face had softened. "I asked Tracy if anyone had been in asking about you, or if she had told anyone that you were staying at Jess's house."

A lead ball of anxiety dropped into her stom-ach. She had told Tracy where she was stay-ing and hadn't thought to mention that the girl should keep it to herself, so if that was how the man today had found her, then that meant it was her fault it had happened. Her fault Jess and Seth's home had been damaged. Her fault that Miles had nearly gotten shot protecting her. "You're telling me that she did tell some-one?"

Please say no.

He nodded. She wasn't surprised, but her mouth suddenly felt as if she had swallowed cot-ton. "She claims a man came in late last night, right before she closed, claiming to be a friend of your brother's," he signed. "He asked if you were working, and said he had stopped by your apartment to see you, but you weren't there. He was worried. She told him you were fine, but staying at Jess's. She didn't think anything of it, because he didn't ask for the address, just smiled and left."

"If she gave Jess's last name, he could have looked it up," she signed, feeling hollow inside.

He brushed her shoulder. "If he was working with someone who knows you—knows where you live and who your friends are—he wouldn't need to have her last name."

Working with someone who knows her? That would make sense. Although the idea that someone she knew could be helping the man targeting her was terrifying.

Questions bubbled to the surface. She welcomed them, as they replaced the panic that was circling, waiting for the opportunity to pounce. Before she could ask them, another officer arrived. Miles introduced him as Sergeant Ryan Parker. He seemed like a nice enough man. Certainly, there was nothing alarming about the handsome officer, with his brown eyes, friendly grin and close-cut auburn hair.

But he wasn't Miles. As Miles left her in the sergeant's care, she straightened her shoulders and went to work, stocking shelves and filling online orders. She couldn't shake the feeling that something bad was about to happen.

Lord, I surrender this day to Your care, she prayed.

Miles dropped the phone back onto the holder, then sat back in his chair. Pushing off with his feet, he tipped back his chair, bringing the front legs off the floor. He swept his hands through his hair.

His suspicions had been confirmed. Somehow, it brought very little comfort.

He rocked his chair, ignoring the sharp squeaks of protest the chair emitted. What did he know? Mentally, he began adding up the facts and events from the past few days.

"Olsen? You planning on buying a new chair when that one breaks?" The smooth drawl slammed into his consciousness, breaking him off midthought. The wheels of his chair crashed against the floor with a hard clatter.

Chief Kennedy stood before him, a quizzical half smile on his face. Miles felt like a kid caught with his hand in the cookie jar. Or possibly a kid who'd been caught trying to sneak a snake into his bedroom. Which he'd done. To his grandmother's horror.

"Sir!" He faced his chief. "Just thinking about

the case. I had a few suspicions. And I'm just about positive that they just got confirmed. I got a little wrapped up in my thoughts."

The chief dipped his chin. "It happens. Want to tell me what you've come up with so far?"

Glad that he wasn't going to hear more about the chair, Miles proceeded to give the chief an overview of the events of the case.

"And we are sure that Gleason had nothing to do with any of these attacks?"

Something in the chief's voice made Miles sit up straighter. The chief wasn't doubting him. He was seriously wanting to hear Miles's thoughts and conclusions. As if he valued them.

"I just got off the phone with the warden of the prison where he was being held. He passed away almost a year ago. Cancer. The first attack—on Ashley—happened recently."

"What're you figurin'?"

Miles leaned back again and swiveled his chair slightly, back and forth, as he collected his thoughts. "Well, it's definitely not playing out as a copycat situation. The attacks and murders aren't following any pattern. At least not that I can tell. The only connection is the fact the people attacked were all survivors from Gleason's final binge. The ones who sent him to jail. This is personal. It feels like vengeance. But by who?" Unable to keep still, he got up and paced a few feet from the desk before turning to face the chief again. In his mind, he was ticking through the facts he knew.

"Does Gleason have any kin? Or did he have a significant other? Someone who could be carrying a grudge?" the chief asked.

Miles shook his head. He'd wondered the same thing. "No, sir. No hint of any relationships. Nor any kin that would want to hurt these girls. He was an only child of two only children. He was three when they adopted him. His conviction devastated them, but they never denied his guilt. Or theirs. I spoke with them just a few minutes before you arrived. They said he was in and out of trouble all his life, filled with anger and a sense of having been wronged. In their words, he felt the world owed him something." Sighing, he ran a hand through his hair. "He was almost nineteen. They decided to take a cruise, so they left him on his own for three weeks. His mother didn't want to. Didn't trust him. But they thought if they gave him some responsibility, it would force him to mature a bit."

Miles popped back down into his chair and scooted to his desk. Where had he put the paper? Yep. That's the one. He snatched up the notes he'd taken and read through.

"These are my notes from the prison warden. Gleason insisted until the day he died that the girls were at fault for what happened. It turns out he did know them. At least he knew Ashley and Jasmine."

"Check in to that. Also, let's widen our search. Do we know who visited him in prison?"

"The list is being sent to me, sir."

Chief Kennedy pursed his lips, deep in thought. "So out of the five young women Gleason abducted, two are dead and one is unconscious. You are keeping watch over Miss Miller. What do we know of the last girl?"

He was ready for that one. "Brooke Cole. Out of the country right now. Her family knows to beware."

The chief nodded, his dark eyes shadowed. "Good plan. If everything works out, we can catch this guy before she comes home. You're doing a fine job, Olsen. A fine job."

Miles felt his eyes widening. Something tight in him relaxed. He had been waiting a long time to hear those words. Words he had feared would never come his way after his gaffe. Even now, almost three years later, he couldn't believe that he had allowed his grief and anger to sap him of his self-control and good sense.

When his stepsister, Sylvie, had been killed, his stepmother had been devastated. The trial and conviction of the woman they all believed to be guilty had brought some closure—but that closure was shattered when Melanie Swanson was released from prison just a few years later. The public hadn't been happy with her release and there were threats and vandalism—even an attack on Melanie's aunt. Enough violent activity to get her police protection, which had included Miles.

Driven by his worry for his stepmother, and his anger over his stepsister's death, he'd taken the opportunity to sneak in some anonymous harassment of his own, hoping that Melanie would get fed up and decide to leave LaMar Pond once and for all, letting them all finally put Sylvie's death behind them. He hadn't known—none of them had—that Sylvie's death hadn't been Melanie's fault at all. That she'd been framed, and that the same people who had ruined her life and gotten her thrown in jail were also trying to kill her once she was released.

Everything had ended well. The real criminals had been caught and imprisoned. Melanie had gotten through her ordeal and had fallen in love with one of her police officer protectors. They were happily married now. But the knowledge that everything worked out didn't take away Miles's feelings of guilt over what he'd done. He was reminded of it every time he saw Lieutenant Tucker. How that man tolerated him after what he had done to his wife was beyond Miles's comprehension.

Clearing his throat, he swiveled to face the chief again. "Thank you, sir."

The chief glanced at the clock on the wall. "Why don't you finish up and go get Miss Miller? Her shift is almost done. I think you are the best man for the job of protecting her right now."

"Okay. Give me about twenty minutes to finish up here, then I'll head out."

"Keep me posted." Whistling, the chief strolled away. Why was it always *The Andy Griffith Show* theme song? He'd be hearing it in his mind all day now.

He grabbed the bottle of Mountain Dew sitting on his desk and took a long swig. He put down the bottle and wiped his mouth, then set about making some more phone calls. Half an hour later, he felt he had accomplished all he could do there.

Flipping his wrist over to see the time, he noted he still had time to get to the bookstore before Rebecca's shift ended. He gathered up his keys and finished off the Mountain Dew before tossing the bottle in the recyclables can. He tapped his watch, bringing up Rebecca's contact information, and sent her a text to let her know he was on his way. It was only polite. Plus, he didn't want her to worry if she saw him pull up when he'd said he would talk with her tomorrow.

He was in his vehicle two minutes later, and there was still no response. Which could mean nothing, he told himself. Not everyone was attached to their phones. When he sent a text to Parker and got no response, though, he couldn't ignore the voice that told him the situation was off.

His pager crackled. The dispatcher's voice broke through the static. "Suspected high-level carbon-monoxide event at 309 Main Street, A Novel Idea Bookstore, with multiple victims."

Fear clenched his heart like a fist. Rebecca was there! Miles flipped on his siren, and peeled away from the curb. Cars pulled to the side as he whizzed past. He switched on his own radio and yelled, "LaMar Pond PD unit six en route to the scene."

Why didn't Parker respond? As a police officer, he should have been aware of the situation before it became critical and started to evacuate the premises. Unless there was more going on than just a carbon-monoxide poisoning.

There was no way this was accidental.

The dispatcher acknowledged his call. Then repeated the call for the local volunteer fire departments to respond. It was the middle of the day. On a beautiful Saturday. He knew from experience that in the rural areas responses might be slower. And he also knew it would take twenty minutes for the local ambulance to arrive. He was Rebecca's best hope.

Please, Lord Jesus, help me be on time.

There was an empty parking space across the street from the store. He parallel-parked, then leaped from his car, running across the street as soon as it was clear. A couple of older customers milled around outside of the store, concern etched on their wrinkled faces. A cursory glance into the window made his heart rate spike. No one was in view. And he knew that there was a minimum of three people who were supposed to be in that store and who were unaccounted for.

"Ladies! Is anyone in there?"

"Yes, officer." One of the women stepped forward. "We were in there and saw the girl at the counter fall down. She didn't move. Then Margie here said she felt funny." She pointed to the other woman.

Miles switched his gaze to Margie. "Are you all right, ma'am?"

"Yes. My son is an EMT for East Mead township. I know the signs of carbon-monoxide poisoning, so we came out and called 911. There were two other people in the store, but I didn't see them when we left."

"We tried to move the lady behind the counter," the other woman interrupted her. "She was too heavy for us."

Miles thanked them and ran to the entrance. He grabbed the door handle and swung the door open, flipping the mechanism at the top of the door to hold it open.

"Ladies," he said to the women outside, "I need to go into the store and start bringing people out. When the paramedics arrive, you need to let them know that there are at least three people inside, four including me. This door needs to remain open so the fumes can begin to air out."

He waited just long enough to receive a nod of agreement, then dashed inside. As he passed the checkout counter, he could see a pale arm stretched out behind the edge of the counter. He recognized the charm bracelet on the slim wrist as the one that Tracy had been wearing earlier that day. Still no sign of Rebecca. Panic rocketed inside him, but he forced himself to push it down. Unfortunately, there was a book cart jammed up against the counter. Not a very safe place for it. Jumping over the counter, he stepped to Tracy's head, and bent down to hook his hands under her armpits. Moving backward, he pulled the unconscious woman out from behind the counter, shoving the book cart out of his way with his hip until he could pick her up. He paused long enough to take the decorative scarf off Tracy's neck and wrap it over his face. He knew it wouldn't provide that much protection, but maybe it would provide just enough for him to do the job.

All the while, Rebecca and Parker were still unaccounted for. *Dear Lord*, he prayed. *Guide me. Help me find them before it's too late.*

What if it was already too late? He couldn't go there. He just could not face the sense of failure he would experience if he let her down. Why did he agree to let her go to work?

A wail split the air. An ambulance was parking up against the curb, its siren wailing. The two paramedics exited, one of them immediately going to Tracy and the customers to check on their condition and start them on oxygen. The other one was holding a handheld carbon-monoxide tester. As soon as he stepped into the building, the tester started beeping. Paling, the young man read the results. "Over eight hundred parts per million! That's almost impossible. Anyone inside is in immediate danger. This level of poisoning acts quickly. Unconsciousness within two hours, death within three!"

"There are still two more people inside, but I couldn't see them! One of them is deaf, so calling out for her won't do any good, even if she's still conscious."

A second emergency vehicle pulled in across the street. Good. But they were still not exiting quickly enough for his peace of mind.

Miles bolted back through the door, ignoring the paramedic who bellowed after him to stop. He should wait, let someone else go in who had protective gear and hadn't already been exposed. But he couldn't be sure there was time, not with two people missing.

This was life and death.

NINE

Miles ran through the bookstore, searching every nook and cranny. He peered around every case as he passed it. Nothing. He began to cough. He knew that the scarf wouldn't provide that much protection. He had hoped it would give him a little more time, though. Reaching the back of the store, he took hold of the doorknob and turned it, pushing the door open with more force than was required. The door slammed against the back wall and bounced back, hitting his shoulder as he charged through it. He barely noticed. All his attention was focused on the scene before him.

Parker was unconscious against the wall, blood dripping from a wound on his head. Given the angle he was at, it was highly unlikely his injury had happened as a result of a fall. More likely, he had interrupted the attacker and had been bludgeoned into unconsciousness. Beyond him lay Rebecca. For one terrifying second, he thought she had stopped breathing. No. Her breaths were erratic and shallow, but he could see her chest rising and falling.

A paramedic burst through the door, followed by an EMT. They nodded as Miles went to Rebecca. Between the two men, they managed to get Parker off the floor and carry him out, going through the back door instead of retracing their steps through the gas-filled store. Good idea.

Muttering a prayer of thanksgiving under his breath, he bent down and lifted the unconscious woman in his arms. Her face was so pale. *Do your job*, he reminded himself.

Miles followed the paramedic and EMT out the back door into the alley. The ambulance was being moved to the back. He stood by as Parker, Tracy and Rebecca were checked and hooked to oxygen. They were all breathing, although none of them regained consciousness.

The paramedic insisted on checking him out, too. He endured the examination as patiently as he could, but all he wanted was to make sure Rebecca, Tracy and Parker were safe.

Within minutes, the three victims were all loaded into ambulances and carried off to the hospital. Miles waited only long enough to see the ambulance carrying Rebecca pull out into traffic on Main Street, sirens blaring, before putting a call into Chief Kennedy to tell him what had been found. Not that that's what he wanted to do. No, indeed. Every instinct inside of him was screaming for him to hop in his car and follow the ambulance to the hospital. But he knew he had to contact his chief first. It made it easier knowing that Jackson had responded to his 911 call and was already en route to the hospital. He would look out for Rebecca until Miles arrived.

"Has a cause been determined?" Chief Kennedy's voice was quiet, but it ran deep with concern.

"Yes, Chief. This was no accident. The furnace had been sabotaged, and the carbon-monoxide alarm was discarded on the ground near where Parker was found. Which is right next to the basement stairs. My guess is Parker had heard the intruder as he attempted to leave through the back door."

"Not a very skilled assassin. He left a witness."

Miles winced. He had thought the same thing. "From the angle of the blow, it's possible that Parker never saw the attacker. And I highly doubt he thought anyone would survive. The level of toxin in the air was shocking. The paramedics said that level of gas could kill within a short time. This was definitely premeditated. I also think it's suspicious that both attacks happened as the owner is conveniently out of the way."

"In your opinion, she's a link. Or a suspect."

Miles nodded, then realized the chief couldn't see him. "Yeah. I'm leaning more toward the idea that our attacker knows her. From the description Rebecca gave me the other day, she's not big enough to have been the attacker herself. Nor did Rebecca know anything of her before she opened the bookstore. Chief, I would like to request that both Tracy and Parker be guarded. At least until they are capable of looking out for themselves."

A heavy sigh drifted over the connection. "I figured. Of course, we'll do what we can to provide protection. Still, it's always sad to hear about such evil, to willingly kill innocent people like that. This makes the fourth attempt on Miss Miller's life."

As if he could forget it.

"Miles, I think as soon as she is released we need to get her into protective custody."

"I would love to see that happen. But somehow, I don't think she'll go for it."

"Not even with everything that's happened?"

Miles took a moment to consider everything that had happened and what he knew about Rebecca. She had been attacked and was aware of the danger, but he also knew she believed that God was looking out for her. And he also had figured out that her family was of utmost importance to her. She worked so hard to keep those ties, it would devastate her to miss Levi's wedding.

"Sir, her brother's wedding is in five days, on Thursday. I'm pretty sure she will be in the hospital until Monday, so it would be easier to keep an eye on her for now. We can up the security at Seth's for when she gets out. Make sure she is never alone. On the day of the wedding, I will be with her the entire time. I will talk with her about the ceremony. It's important to her, so I will ask her to invite me as her guest." He waited while the chief thought about it.

"I agree that you should be there. Also, I think it would be better for her if she dressed Amish for the wedding."

Was that even allowed, since she had chosen to leave that world behind? He would have to see what could be done. Would she agree? He knew her reasons for leaving the Amish community were very personal.

"Will she go along with that?" Chief Kennedy's voice was filled with skepticism as he echoed Miles's thoughts.

"Does she really have a choice?" Miles shook his head, knowing his words came out a bit stronger and more sarcastic than he had meant them to when speaking to his boss. "Anyway, I think she will do whatever she can to be there. And then afterward, I think we will have a better shot at convincing her to go into hiding. Hopefully, we will find the attacker before too long. And before anyone else gets hurt."

Oh, wait. "Chief, I think it would be safe to say that I won't be able to openly carry a gun at the wedding."

A lengthy pause filled the silence. Miles imagined the chief closing his eyes and pinching the bridge of his nose. "I don't like the sound of that. We'll have to think about it. I would prefer you have a weapon on you, even if it's concealed. You will be on duty, even if you're dressed as a guest. If the killer shows up, we need to be prepared."

Yeah, that could get awkward. Although if the attacker was close enough, Miles felt confident he'd be able to take him down in hand-to-hand combat. He was a black belt in karate, thanks to the need to prove himself capable. One more thing he owed to his parents' dysfunctional relationship.

"Okay, Miles. I think you have a good handle on this. I will put all personnel on notice that they may be called upon for a security detail."

Miles disconnected the call. For a couple of minutes, he stood where he was, running over

the conversation and his options in his mind.
And realized he really didn't have any. He had
to protect Rebecca. And unless she decided to
accept his recommendation that she place herself in protective custody, that meant he had to
attend an Amish wedding. Why was he so nervous about that? He'd attended lots of weddings
before. Lieutenant Willis had gotten married a
year and a half ago and Seth had gotten married just a couple of months ago.

But he knew why this one was different. He
was going there, as an outsider, as Rebecca's
guest. Even if it was for protective purposes,
he would be viewed as if he had a more personal connection with Rebecca. And the worst
of it was, there was a connection. He liked her.
She was smart and funny, and her strength and
sorrow-filled eyes touched his heart.

Which was precisely what worried him.

None of that was important, though. All that
mattered was that he would be there to protect
Rebecca and those she loved from a killer.

Where was she?

Rebecca opened her eyes, squinting as her
head ached in protest. She was connected to a
machine. For someone raised in a small Amish
community with no electricity or modern tech-
nology, the sight should have been unusual,

maybe even upsetting all on its own. Unfortunately, Rebecca had very clear memories of waking up in a hospital before, surrounded by far more frightening-looking machines and monitors, and a crowd of people looking down at her.

Reflexively, she glanced down at her wrists. No rub burns from restraints this time. And though her head hurt, her back and legs didn't feel as though they were on fire. Because no one had been beating her this time, or cutting her. No one had physically assaulted her at all this time…but that didn't mean no one was hurt.

Sergeant Parker.

She needed to find out if he was alive. She had walked into the back room to get something and found him bleeding on the floor. She remembered helping him to sit up—feeling a little woozy and sick herself as she crouched down beside him. He'd tried to tell her something. Maybe some kind of warning, but he had been too weak to make his point understood. She must have blacked out. Or had she been attacked, too?

No. She would have remembered that. Instead, all she remembered was a searing headache before absolute nothing.

The door opened. A nurse entered the room with a cart and smiled. Miles followed her in.

The tightness that had begun to bunch in her shoulders loosened at the sight of his familiar face. He approached the bed and waited as the nurse busied herself with the machine and checking on Rebecca's vitals.

Then she started speaking. Miles positioned himself near the nurse's shoulder and interpreted, reciting the information the nurse offered about how her vitals had stabilized nicely.

"Okay, the doctor should be in shortly," Miles concluded.

One of her hands was still connected to a machine. Rebecca used her free hand to ask what was wrong with her.

"The doctor will explain everything. Don't worry. You're in good hands here."

The nurse wheeled her cart over to the door. Miles beat her there and held the door open. As soon as she left, he closed the door again.

She tried to push herself up to a sitting position, but he placed a firm hand on her shoulder and shook his head. Fine. It was embarrassing talking to him lying down. She felt vulnerable and weak. That didn't matter, though. "Is your friend all right? The officer named Parker?"

Miles leaned in closer. "I just left his room. He will be fine. Probably needs to take a few days off work. But no permanent damage has been done."

Her bones dissolved. At least that's how she felt as she melted back into the mattress, the anxiety festering inside her evaporating. The officer would be well—he hadn't been seriously injured because he'd been protecting her.

"Will you tell me what happened?" She was not in the mood to be placated while she waited for the doctor to make an appearance. All this avoidance of the issue only made her feel worse.

"What do you remember?" Miles moved the lone chair so that they could see each other without being hampered by the tubes and wires. She appreciated the thoughtfulness.

What did she remember? Not enough, that was a fact.

"Not much. I was supposed to change the window display today. I went into the back room to gather what I would need. But I found Sergeant Parker on the floor. He was bleeding, here…" She touched her head with her free hand. "When I kneeled beside him, he opened his eyes and tried to sit up. I didn't think he should, but I couldn't get him to stay still, so I helped him. He seemed agitated, upset. I think he was trying to tell me something. Maybe he thought I could read his lips. I'm sorry. I tried to learn, but I never mastered it…"

Would things have been different if she could?

She noticed Miles looking at her arm. The

scars from when Terry Gleason had cut her for his amusement were thick scarlet slashes on her pale skin.

Would he be repelled by them? She was afraid to look at him.

Miles touched her hand, then caught her gaze as she looked up. His eyes were soft. She could see no sign of disgust. "You can't blame yourself for any of this. What happened next?"

Closing her eyes briefly, she let the images from earlier fill her mind. What happened next? She signed the question in her mind, thinking through the answer.

"I had started to feel sick earlier. And my head was aching. I was getting sleepy. I think my headache got bad really fast. And then, I must have fainted or something. Because the next thing I was aware of was waking up here."

He nodded and leaned back. His normally expressive face was nearly blank. The ultra-controlled expression scared her more than anything else could. It stated without words that the situation had escalated even more. And that there was nothing random about what had happened at the bookstore.

Not that she'd thought there was. Not even for a second.

Miles waved his hand slightly. When she looked at him, he touched his index finger to his chin and made a twisting motion. "Serious." She tensed again. It was a definite statement that something important was coming. "This was no accident. I'm sure you already know that. Someone sabotaged the furnace so that the store was flooded with carbon-monoxide gas. I have to think that Sergeant Parker somehow interrupted the person responsible and that was why he was hit. There was a fire extinguisher on the floor. It had blood on it. That's most likely what the attacker used."

Her breath exploded out of her. Thinking back, she vaguely remembered stepping past the extinguisher. She'd been so worried about Parker that she hadn't given it a second thought.

"He says he went to the back room to do a routine check of the premises, and didn't see anyone. The person must have hidden behind the door leading to the basement stairs until Parker was already in the room. Then *bam*!"

She jumped as he slammed his fist into his palm. She wasn't offended at the graphic description, but her nerves were so strained that any little thing made her jumpy. Miles continued. "He'll be able to leave here tomorrow or Monday so that's good news. Although, that means there will be one less police officer on the job." His brow furrowed as he considered that. Poor Miles. He looked exhausted. "When you are released, I will bring you back to the Travis house. We've increased police protection."

Suddenly, her mind took a detour.

"Wait! Thursday is my brother's wedding! What am I supposed to do about that?" It was unbearable, thinking of missing Levi's special day.

Miles ducked his head slightly, and his shaggy blond hair bobbed on his forehead. "I've been thinking of that. I know that non-Amish people sometimes are guests at weddings. How about if I go with you? To protect you and your family."

She blinked. That was an interesting idea. But a police officer…

"You can't go dressed in your uniform."

He responded with an elaborate eye roll. "Please. Give me some credit. I do own some church clothes. I will do my best not to stand out."

"But you will."

She watched his eyes widen and realized she had probably been too blunt. She hurried to explain. "Sorry. But I have seen you while you work. Your eyes never stop moving. You are constantly looking around for danger. Even while you are laughing, your eyes are moving. The only time they don't is when you are signing to me." She pursed her lips and tilted her head, examining his surprised face.

Miles smiled, an open smile showing straight white teeth. Lovely.

"I won't apologize for that. I plan to keep on my guard to keep you and your family safe." His smile widened even more, becoming a grin, with a touch of smugness to it. "And I think spending a full day in your company will be very enjoyable."

Oh, my. She was aware of something shifting inside of her heart. Keeping a step ahead of a vicious killer wasn't her only problem. No. Now it seemed she also had to keep her heart safe from the man she believed God had sent to protect her.

A short while later, Miles stood and stretched. She averted her eyes when she realized she was watching the play of his biceps under his T-shirt. *Not appropriate, Rebecca.* He yawned, but to her mind it looked exaggerated.

"I need to head out. You okay if I go?" he signed.

No, no, please stay.

"Of course, I will be fine. You go work. Or whatever."

He grinned, his blond hair flopping over his forehead. Her fingers itched to brush the soft hair back. Why was she letting herself get so distracted? Her eyes met his, and the smile slipped from his face. His blue eyes grew intense, and the air between them sizzled. For a moment, she felt breathless, as if the air had grown thin.

He backed up, and the moment faded.

Sketching a brief wave, he sauntered out of the room, though he did turn back and catch her gaze one last time before he left. She had a feeling she'd be reliving that weighted glance and trying to dissect it for the rest of the evening. It was going to be a long sleepless night.

TEN

The next morning, the nurse was just carrying away Rebecca's half-eaten breakfast tray when the door opened. Rebecca's eyes shot wide when her boss, April, entered the room, her face pale and drawn. Normally, April was very well put together. This morning, she was without makeup and her hair had been slapped up in a messy bun. She approached the bed, taking in Rebecca and her surroundings. As she stopped at the bed, she pulled out her phone and tapped a message, then showed it to Rebecca.

R U ok? I just saw Tracy. She'll be fine.

Rebecca took the phone and tapped a message back. I'm fine. I will be going home soon.

April's lips firmed as she read the message. And then she typed a response. I heard about your roommate. I'm so sorry. And Tracy said you were attacked the other night after closing the store. What's going on?

Good question. How to answer it.

She could see Miles's image in her mind, signing to her to be careful, not to give away too much information. It wasn't that she didn't trust April, but her innocent conversation with Tracy, revealing that she was staying with Jess, had shown her it was safer to be vague. The police are looking into it. I don't know too much more than that.

Well, that was true, wasn't it? She really didn't know too much more. Other than the same group of girls she'd been abducted with years before were being hunted down, one by one. But April didn't know anything about that event. And, she realized, she didn't want her to. Didn't want to see her boss start to view her as a victim, to look at her with pity.

Rebecca kept the past to herself. And when April finally left after a few awkward moments, she was relieved.

The rest of the day dragged on. Rebecca hated not being able to get to church, so she comforted herself with watching a service on the TV and praying.

The next morning, she was informed that she was being released.

Rebecca should have been overjoyed. After

all, she hated hospitals. She'd been stuck in one for three days after the abduction, needing constant medical care after being dehydrated and brutally beaten. It wasn't a pleasant memory.

She wasn't happy to be leaving the hospital this time, though. In fact, she was terrified.

She had expected Miles to be here when she was released. But he wasn't. She had no idea where he was. And that made her feel distinctly uneasy. In her mind, she replayed the conversation they had had the night before. He hadn't mentioned being here when she was released. She'd just assumed. Although, they didn't know she would be sprung so quickly.

The nurse entered the room pushing a VRI, a video remote interpreting system. It was a portable device used by hospitals and legal offices to connect with certified interpreters. Personally, Rebecca preferred to have an interpreter physically in the same room. If she needed to go to the doctor or the audiologist, she always made the appointment and scheduled an interpreter well in advance. Clearly, an interpreter wasn't available currently. She sighed, but didn't complain.

The nurse began to explain the release procedures while the interpreter relayed the information to Rebecca.

It was amazing. Brilliant. Incredibly helpful. And yet she felt so alone.

No one was here that she knew. How would she get home? Text Miles? But he was either working, or home enjoying his time off shift, and either way she felt hesitant to disturb whatever it was that he was up to. Because she hated the idea of relying too much on him.

Finally, the efficient nurse shoved some papers under her nose. She was to sign to show she understood. And then she could go.

Great.

As she was finishing up her signature, the door opened. A familiar head popped in, shaggy blond hair flopping to the side due to the angle he was holding his head. Her mood lightened instantly. Caution stirred inside, as well. The nurse smiled at Miles as she left the room.

"Hey." Miles grinned and pulled the rest of himself inside the room. "Your guard outside let me know that you were being released. I was taking a trip today. Thought you might want to come along."

Interest stirred.

"Where?" she signed.

He sauntered closer to her. "The visitor log from the prison arrived this morning. It seems Terry Gleason had only three visitors the entire time he was in prison. His parents and a man by the name of Declan Winters."

"Winters? The same last name as Jasmine?"

He bobbed his head up and down in a slow, exaggerated motion. Even his signs were exaggerated, emphasizing that this was very unusual. "Exactly like Jasmine's. In fact, Declan is her older brother. I want to know why this man was visiting the man who killed his sister on a weekly basis."

Wow. She didn't even know what to say to that.

"So, you want to go? Or should I drop you off at Jess's house? There's someone on guard there at all times now."

"Are you kidding me? Obviously, I'm going with you."

The smirk that graced his face told her he expected her to say that. She didn't care. The idea of going back to the house was unappealing. And going with him would be interesting. Plus, she'd hopefully find out more about what was going on.

But, wasn't there some kind of rule against taking her along on police business? She asked him.

"The chief gave his approval. We're short-staffed at the moment with Parker out of commission. Plus, he thinks that as I am the only one who can sign, it might be beneficial for you to stay with me."

Sounded like a good idea to her.

This was probably the dumbest idea he'd ever had. Taking Rebecca on a police visit? It had made so much sense when he had broached the subject with the chief that morning. But now? Not so much. Not when she was so charming and funny. And her blunt honesty really struck a chord with him.

Seeking something else to focus on, his eyes flicked to the rearview mirror and he noticed that the car behind them had gotten a little too close.

Not again. He tapped on the brakes, and the car fell back. It took a lot of guts or arrogance to tailgate a police car. Was it deliberate? He sped up to see if the car would follow them.

It stayed back, and soon two other cars were between them. Maybe he should consider going on vacation when this case was over. He smirked to himself. He was getting paranoid. But better paranoid than careless. He stopped at a stop sign.

A hand tapped on his arm. He glanced over briefly.

Rebecca signed the word *funny*, scrunching

her eyebrows down in a motion that signaled a "wh" question, meaning "What's so funny?"

He slid his eyes back to the road and answered one-handed as he continued through the intersection. "I'm starting to see things. I thought we were being followed, but it was only my imagination."

He hoped.

Once more he flicked his gaze to the mirror. The car was out of sight. Yep. He needed a vacation.

Between the attraction that simmered between them and the always present concern of being followed, the car ride to Warren, where Declan Winters resided, was rife with enough tension that he half expected the air to start crackling with it. He rather suspected that was why their arrival at Winters's house seemed so anticlimactic.

No need to wonder if Winters was home. The man himself stood outside in his driveway, his expression intent as he used a circular saw on a two-by-four laid across two sawhorses. He stopped sawing as they pulled in. When he bent down and unplugged the tool before removing his safety glasses, Miles silently approved. You never left equipment plugged in when it wasn't in use.

"Declan Winters?" Miles asked as he left his

vehicle. Rebecca remained in the car, as he'd instructed. He didn't want her out in the open until he knew it was safe. She was better off where he could keep an eye on her and keep her out of harm's way at the same time.

"Yeah? That's me." The tall man standing behind his makeshift workplace narrowed his gaze, letting it drift to the badge and the name. "What can I do for you, Officer Olsen? Do you have more information about my sister?"

Miles quirked an eyebrow. "Your sister?"

The man waved, like he was swatting a fly. "Yeah. I assumed this was about Jazzy again."

"Because?"

"Some reporter left a message on my machine, wanting to discuss her kidnapping and murder. I never responded." Now the man grew cautious. "If you're not here about my sister, what's this about?"

Give a little. Maybe he'll open up more about his sister.

"Mr. Winters, are you aware that the women who were abducted with your sister ten years ago have recently been targeted?"

"Targeted?" Declan paled. He shook his head. "Targeted how?"

"Targeted as in abducted and beaten. One of them is in a coma in the hospital. Another is dead. A third has been attacked, but escaped."

"It's not Terry Gleason. He's dead. I know because I visited him every week for years."

Miles smiled. His instinct told him the man was on the level. "I know. Why? He killed your sister."

Declan straightened, hands behind his back, a fierce scowl appearing. Not at Miles. He appeared to be struggling with himself. Miles had a sudden picture in his mind of Dan Willis, standing in a similar posture. Dan was ex-military. The file had mentioned that Declan had been in the navy.

Following his instincts, Miles suggested they move to a more secure location, less in the open. Like the garage. When Declan agreed, he moved to the cruiser to get Rebecca. She exited the vehicle, her posture tight. She seemed ready to bolt, and he waved her ahead of himself, using his body as a buffer for whatever dangers might be out there.

His shoulder blades twitched. He ignored it, just motioned her to move faster. She didn't ask questions, just quickened her gentle gait until she was inside the relative safety of the garage walls. He pushed past her to grab the large door and pull it closed. Well, that wasn't helpful. The door was cut into three sections, and almost the entire top section consisted of three rectangular windows. He found himself as close to growling as he had ever come. How was he supposed to keep Rebecca safe in these conditions?

No one knew she was here, he reasoned. Still, caution was the word of the day. He signed to her to move to the side of the garage for safety, voicing it aloud for Declan's benefit.

Declan shrugged, and got his first clear look at Rebecca. His jaw dropped.

"Hey! I remember you! You were at the trial!"

Funny how some things stayed in your mind.

Miles quickly signed introductions. He made sure to sign everything in pidgin. "We were discussing why you went to visit your sister's murderer in prison. I would have expected you to be angry at him."

Declan rubbed the back of his neck with one hand, the other hand set loosely on his hip. "It's odd, I know. After the trial, I was bitter. Yeah, Gleason went to jail, but my baby sister was still dead. My parents couldn't handle the stress. They split. Both of them have remarried. My mom still can't celebrate Mother's Day. It practically destroyed my family. So yeah, I was angry. Beyond angry. I was at rock bottom. And then I met someone who taught me to see it all through faith. It didn't happen overnight. It took a good year for me to get to a place of forgiveness."

"Forgiveness?" Miles jerked a little at that. He was a Christian, and he still felt hostility rearing in his soul whenever his stepsister's murderer was mentioned. Yet this guy was talking about forgiveness.

"Yeah, forgiveness. It's not easy. But it was necessary. You gotta understand—bitterness was eating me alive. I could feel it destroying me from the inside out."

Miles nodded. He had experienced the same feeling.

"I forgave Gleason, not because he needed it, but because I did. And then I became an outreach minister at my church. When the program moved into the prison system, I knew I was being called to go there."

A gentle nudge pushed at his conscience. He knew he was supposed to forgive those who wronged him, but did that really extend to murderers?

Father, forgive them, for they know not what they do. How many times had he heard that Scripture? It had always made him faintly uncomfortable. Yes, he knew he needed to forgive. Allowing the bitterness inside him to fester had almost cost him his job once. By letting it remain, he was risking letting it cost him even more.

A warm hand crept into his, squeezing gently. Rebecca. "Are you okay?" she signed one-handed. *No. But I'm gonna be. Father, help me to forgive and move on.*

"I'm fine. Thanks," he signed back. And returned his attention to Declan.

"Was Gleason receptive?"

Declan shook his head. "Not really. He was very angry. Apparently, he knew a few of the girls from school. He was a year behind, so he graduated when he was almost nineteen. From what he said, they were pretty and popular and took delight in tormenting him. At least, that's his side of the story. I think he tolerated my visits because they gave him an outlet to vent his anger. That, and no one else came to visit him."

"I know he had no family aside from his parents," Miles began, but stopped short when Declan shook his head.

"He had an older brother."

What? He quickly signed the statement to Rebecca.

"A brother!" Rebecca signed, jumping into the conversation for the first time, eyes opened wide.

Miles knew just how she felt. "His file lists him as an only child."

"An *adopted* only child," Declan amended. "He had a biological half brother somewhere that he lived with until he was three. The brother was five. When his birth mother was killed, the brother was sent to live with his birth father, who refused to take Terry because Terry was no relation to him. Terry was adopted by a well-meaning couple who thought it was cruel that the brothers were separated. So they made sure Terry knew about him. I know Terry always intended on finding his brother someday. But he died before he could."

"He never met him after they were separated as kids?" Miles tapped all the information into his notes app. Later, he'd email it to himself so he could make out a report and a list of details he needed to check. Just to give himself a clear picture of all the connections in the case.

"Not that I'm aware of."

It was enough to make a man crazy.

"Do you have a name for this brother? A physical description? Anything?"

Declan shook his head. "Sorry. All I know is that he was two years older."

Just when he'd thought they were getting somewhere. Was it possible that his brother had come looking for Terry—or for revenge on the people who had put Terry away? Miles's mind whirled at the implications. He needed to start looking for this brother. Because he had the feeling the brother had already found them.

Miles opened his mouth to thank Declan for his time. But never got the chance. The window next to him blew apart, showering all three of them with glass. Almost immediately, the sound of more glass breaking echoed from outside. A car window. Miles dove for Rebecca. So did Declan. Between the two men, she was hidden from view of whoever was shooting.

Miles wasn't. He was well aware that he had just made himself a breathing target.

ELEVEN

Hunched between two muscular men, Rebecca couldn't even get enough air to scream. The middle window blew apart. She flinched. Miles pulled her in closer to him. Her forehead was pressed up against his neck. She could feel his pulse racing.

She drew in a deep breath—his clean scent came with it, bringing comfort. And security.

And fear.

What was he doing? If she raised her head to look over his shoulder, she knew she'd have a clear view of the windows. Which meant someone looking in could see her. And would literally have to go through Miles to get her. And maybe Declan, too, she realized. Whoever was after her was relentless, and seemed to be growing braver by the hour, so she had little doubt that he would shoot other people to get to her.

She did her best to pull back from Miles, so he could find shelter, too. But he wouldn't let her. Instead, those strong arms tightened, drawing her closer. There was nothing to do but wait it out.

And pray.

Rebecca lifted her mind to God, and in her mind, she signed to Him, asking for safety, for all three of them, and for Brooke and Ashley. She prayed that the killer would be found. And then, she paused. Slowly, she sent another prayer, asking for her attacker's redemption. It felt strange, but she knew, after learning Declan's story, that it was the right thing to do. The memory of Miles's shattered expression as he'd listened to Declan burst into her mind.

There was a story there. An anguish that he kept hidden. If they got out of this alive... No. *When* they escaped this situation, she'd ask him. He knew her history. She wanted to know what haunted him.

Her right leg was starting to go numb from being crouched in an awkward position for so long. Abruptly, Miles released her, catching her again as she started to stumble back.

"Sorry," he signed. "I can hear sirens outside. One of the neighbors must have called the police."

She nodded and straightened painfully. Standing was difficult, as pins and needles attacked her right leg. "My leg went to sleep," she signed in apology, clutching at Miles's arm for balance.

He grinned, the unexpected expression sending her heartbeat skittering, but the look was gone in a flash, replaced by his cop face. Which was probably why she nearly fell over as he leaned in quickly and kissed her forehead. "You're okay, right? Anything hurt?"

"Fine," she signed, wishing she could stem the tide of warmth spreading through her face. The man was making her melt like a gooey marshmallow. Not good.

"You okay?" He addressed Declan.

She melted some more. Except for police business, even when he wasn't talking to her, he remembered to sign, to include her in the conversation. Her own family didn't do that. Couldn't, she reminded herself.

She broke out of her thoughts when Miles jerked back. "Police are at the door." He strode to the main door and looked through the broken windows, then yelled out, continuing to sign for her benefit, "Hold up your badge, please." She could see his body relax slightly before he opened the door.

"Could you two remain here, please?" he asked Declan and Rebecca. They both nodded.

She understood. He wanted to make sure everything was safe. As much as she hated not being able to see him, she knew he had a job to do. And she couldn't keep him from it.

It struck her just how dangerous his job was. Her heart was becoming attached to him, but she didn't know if she was happy with that. After the abduction ten years ago, she'd wanted safety. She had lived through enough fear. She didn't know if she was strong enough to go through more. Giving her heart to a policeman meant watching that heart walk into danger every day. Could she live with that?

But then, wasn't she living through it now? She'd been surrounded by danger ever since the attacks had begun. And she wasn't falling apart. God would help her through whatever situation she was in.

He'd done it before.

It felt like forever until Miles returned. The tension inside her escalated. What if it was a trick? What if he was out there in danger? The thought that she would be next also popped up, but she shoved that aside. Because right at the moment, Miles was what mattered. The one thing that helped was that Declan was so calm, knowing that he could hear some of what was happening outside. She could see him cock his head several times, listening. He sent her a small smile. It didn't send her heart racing like Miles's did, but it comforted her. Surely, the man wouldn't be smiling if he thought a murderer was about to charge through the door and finish them off. Right?

Just when she thought she could not stand the strain one more minute, Miles popped his head back through the door. His shaggy hair was going in all directions, as if he'd been running a frustrated hand through it. Many times. She tucked the corners of her mouth in, hoping to keep her smile from peeping through. Judging by the way he squinted at her, she wasn't totally successful. He shrugged, and waved at them to come out.

Two police cars were in front of Declan's driveway. At least fifteen people dotted the street, craning their necks to get a full view of everything. It was probably the most excitement this small town had seen in a while. It was natural that they would be curious. Still, she ducked her head, uncomfortable with the scrutiny. Miles, she noted, did his best to keep himself between the crowd and her, shielding her from prying eyes and any dangers that might come flying at them.

Again, a smile threatened. It died completely when she saw Miles's cruiser. She gasped. The side passenger window and the windshield were shattered. Another bullet had gone through the driver's door. She knew without being told that they wouldn't be driving back to LaMar Pond like that. It was going to be a long day.

"Why shoot the car?" she signed to Miles, having trouble processing what she was seeing.

"It was in the way." He kept his face blank, but she sensed there was rage beneath the surface. She shivered. "He must have been over there—" he waved vaguely to the left "—and was trying to get to us in the garage. I assume he didn't care who or what he hit."

The local police were questioning a woman about her mother's age. The woman motioned down the street, then swung her arm in an outward arc toward the other side. When her finger was pointing at Declan's house, she acted like she was aiming a gun at the garage. Then she jerked it back. *Bang, bang.* Rebecca could see it clearly in her head. Then the woman moved her arm and pointed toward the opposite end of the street.

Miles moved to stand beside her. Uh-oh. His jaw was cranked so tight, she thought it would shatter if she touched it. A muscle jumped on the right side. Something the woman said was eating at him. What?

Finally, the officer nodded and the woman drifted off. Miles turned to her. "The gist of that conversation is that the woman noticed a car driving down the street. Three, four times.

Each time it got to this house, the driver would slow down. All she could see for sure was that he was wearing a dark hoodie, and the hood was up. The last time he went past, he opened fire."

"Why would he risk firing with witnesses around?" It didn't make any sense.

"There were no witnesses outside. She was upstairs in her sewing room, and just happened to be facing the window. He probably didn't realize she could see him."

Okay. That made sense. "So, what else is wrong? You're a lot more upset than you were ten minutes ago." And that was saying something, because he was plenty upset then.

He started.

Yeah, busted, she thought, but kept it to herself.

"I'm mad at myself mostly. You and Declan are in more danger, because of me."

She tilted her head, trying to make sense of that. "I don't see that. You didn't shoot at us."

He paced away, then turned and faced her. The torment in his blue eyes just about ripped her heart out. "But I should have trusted my gut more. I am almost one-hundred-percent sure the shooter was in that car I thought was following us earlier."

How to handle this? She was beginning to realize that her protector had a very sensitive soul. One that had been wounded before. He was also the kind of man to shoulder the blame for everything himself. She didn't want to add to the guilt she could see weighing him down.

"How could you have known?" she signed. "Once he realized he'd been spotted, he turned off before we could get a good look at him. You can't see the future. Only God can. I think instead of blaming yourself, you should be praising Him. I am. He knew that there would be danger today, and sent me someone who would know how to keep me safe when it happened."

He shrugged. But his lips curled upward. She sighed, some of the ache dissipating.

"I feel bad about him, though." Miles jerked a thumb over his shoulder at Declan, who was still talking to the police. "He is going to take a leave of absence from work and go out of town. He's in danger now. I think our interest in him has put him on the hit list."

Another person in harm's way.

"He might have been in danger anyway," she argued. "Didn't you say he was Terry Gleason's last visitor? Maybe that's why the shooter was so willing to kill him."

The lips that were still curled bloomed into a full smile, filled with wonder. Her breath caught in her throat. Stunning.

"You are amazing, do you know that?"

"Thanks," she signed, flushing. Accepting praise was not her strong point. Deflection, however, was. "Do you think it was Gleason's brother?"

He cast her a glance that clearly said she wasn't fooling him.

After a moment, he nodded. "I do. I can't prove it yet. But I need to find out as much as I can about the brother. Which means we need to get back to LaMar Pond."

She prayed with all her might that he would find the brother. Too many people were in danger. And she knew life wouldn't get back to normal, for any of them, until whoever was responsible was stopped.

Would this nightmare ever end?

This was getting out of control.

Miles tightened his grip on the steering wheel and clenched his teeth until his jaw ached. He forced himself to relax. No sense letting himself get riled up. He couldn't afford to let his judgment get clouded.

Speaking of that...

He angled his head until he had a clear view of Rebecca, fast asleep in the passenger seat. Poor woman. She was exhausted. They'd had to wait around for two hours until the glass repair people had come and fixed the broken windows. He'd have to wait to get the damage done to the actual door repaired, but at least the car was drivable again.

Rebecca had conked out soon after they had left, giving him time to think.

And worry. He was getting too attached to Rebecca. He knew it. Had known it as soon as he realized how anxious he was at leaving her alone inside the garage to talk to the other police officers. Okay, so Declan was there, and the man looked like he knew how to take care of himself. But Miles hated trusting Rebecca's safety to anyone else.

Getting emotionally involved was a bad thing. Hadn't he learned his lesson when his mom left, nearly destroying his dad? Or, even more recently, when he'd let his judgment get skewed enough to act like some vigilante?

Reflexively, he moved one hand to his shoulder, where his sergeant insignia had once been. He shouldn't complain. It was his own fault he'd been reduced in rank. It could have been worse. The chief would have been justified in firing him altogether. Miles knew that. He was humbled and grateful for the opportunity to prove himself.

An opportunity he could easily mess up again if he allowed his feelings to interfere.

Not just that, he realized. If his feelings got in

the way, it could keep him from seeing a threat or a clue. Someone could get hurt because of him. Rebecca could get hurt.

Or worse.

Time to man up, Miles. This isn't the time for a relationship.

They were almost back to LaMar Pond. He hated to disturb her, but knew he needed to. He waited until the last minute, though. Finally, as he parked the car outside of Seth's house, he had to wake her.

He reached out a hand and gently shook her.

Screeching like a scalded cat, she shot up in her seat, hands out in front as if she was ready to fight. The seat belt pulled her up short. He watched the realization of where she was sink in. And grinned as she slumped back into her seat, glaring.

Trying to wipe the grin from his face, he leaned up against the door, hands raised. He started to sign. A laugh spluttered from him. Her glare intensified, lids lowering until her eyes were almost slits. She was adorable.

"Sorry! You're back at Seth and Jess's house. It was time for you to wake up." No matter how hard he tried, he couldn't squelch the chuckles that kept coming. His shoulders shook with the effort to hold them back. It was most likely the stress of the past few days catching up with him.

He was about to issue another apology, worried that he'd really offended her, when her lips started to twitch.

"Fine. Whatever. Do you want to come in for a cup of coffee?"

He shouldn't. He really shouldn't. "Yeah, sure."

So, of course he did. He rolled his eyes at himself when she got out of the car.

He looked around and frowned. "Is anyone else here?" She swiveled her head around in surprise. All the cars were gone.

Raising his watch, he saw he had missed several messages. And an alert. He must have switched it to mute by accident. Of all the times for that to happen.

"Hold on," he signed. "I have several messages."

"Let's go inside, I will fix coffee, and you can check your messages."

Made sense. He nodded and followed her inside the house, then did a walk-through to make sure everything was secure. Then he joined her in the kitchen. While she busied herself making coffee, he read through his messages. His alarm grew with each message.

By the time she sat down across from him with two mugs, his nerves were buzzing, making sitting still difficult.

"What's wrong?" she signed.

Of course, she'd pick up on the body language. One thing was for sure, he'd never be able to lie to her. Not that he ever would—he'd learned that deception was a very poor choice.

"I have messages from Seth, the chief, Jackson…everyone! There was a fire at the LaMar Pond Senior Center. Residents need to be evacuated. Seth is there. He says he dropped Jess off at his sister Maggie's house."

"Oh, no!" she signed. "Was anyone injured?"

He tapped his watch to view the message that was just coming in. And grimaced. "Yes. Multiple injuries, from mild to severe. And two residents died. One of the residents who died was Sergeant Zee's grandmother. She's going to need to help her family deal with this situation."

"You need to go." It wasn't a question. Her signs were calm, rational, giving him permission to go do his job.

But he could sense the fear. She couldn't lie to him, either.

"I need to go, but I won't leave you unattended. Seth won't be back until all the residents have been checked over. Nor do we have an extra police officer to spare to guard you right now. Let me think."

She waited, sipping her coffee. He paced the

room. Where would she be safe until this crisis was over? Then it hit him.

"Come on. I'm taking you to stay with my family. My grandparents and uncle live less than half an hour from here."

"Will I be safe there?"

A valid question. "I believe you will. No one will know you're there except for those I tell. And my uncle and grandfather both know how to handle a gun. Plus, I know they have a security system in place. It made sense, because they're all deaf."

Some of the fear seemed to melt away. He got it. The possibility of being unable to communicate was part of what scared her. That would not be a problem at his grandparents' house. Even the majority of their guests were skilled signers.

It took her only a few minutes to gather together her things and get ready. Within forty-five minutes they were pulling into his grandparents' driveway.

As he'd expected, his family and grandparents were delighted to have her stay with them. Sally and Bruce Olsen were the kind of people who never turned anyone out. And his uncle Greg lived to entertain others. The fact that he was completely deaf had never stood in his way.

For a moment, Miles was struck by how different the rest of his family was from him and his father. And not just in the fact that they couldn't hear, either. The rest of the family was open and embraced life and people. Miles's father, on the other hand, had allowed bitterness to taint everything he did. And Miles? He didn't think he was bitter, but he sure wasn't as accepting as the others.

"I will come back later. Is it okay if I take the couch for the night?"

"Of course!" his gran signed. The smile she beamed at him was the best guilt trip ever. It was filled with joy. And gratitude. As if him coming to stay with them was an unexpected gift. He needed to stop by more often. When had he become too busy to visit his family? Before the guilt could swamp him too much, she continued. "I will leave the front porch light on. And something to eat in the refrigerator."

Where was Rebecca? She had disappeared with his uncle while he had talked with his grandparents. He should say goodbye.

Why? She knew where he was going. It wasn't like she was his girl.

He wished she was. That rocked him off balance. When had she become so important to him? The emotional tug he felt toward her had sneaked up and sunk its claws into his heart without his even being aware just how deep he was falling.

But he didn't have to act on it. Everyone would be better off if he stopped thinking about Rebecca and refocused on the job. Because that was what he was good at.

Giving his gran a kiss, he walked out the door without seeking out Rebecca.

Hours later, Miles let himself back into the house. It was dark outside. He had expected to find everyone asleep. So he was astounded to find Rebecca sitting up waiting for him at the kitchen table.

The moment she spotted him, she stood and yawned. Then she walked over to him and wrapped her arms around him. He enfolded her in his arms before recalling he was going to keep his distance. Now that he held her, though, he was powerless to let her go. The scent of her shampoo was just what he needed to soothe his frazzled nerves.

Finally, he pulled back and allowed himself to drink in her tired face. Wow, those eyes were the bluest he'd ever seen. Had she slept at all? Dark circles bruised the delicate skin beneath them.

"Everything okay?" he signed, wondering why his grandparents hadn't contacted him if something was amiss.

"Fine. But I was worried. You were gone for

so long. All I could think of is what if my attacker went after you because of me."

She moved back. He let his arms drop, immediately missing her.

So he took a step back, too.

They had no future. He had to remember that. The turmoil that gnawed at him made him want to yell. He needed a workout. A bout with his karate sensei. Anything to relieve his anguish.

"Your grandma and uncle showed me some pictures."

His heart dropped. Instinctively, he knew what pictures she was talking about.

"Sylvie?"

She nodded, her face shadowed. Yes, she understood it was a painful memory.

Rubbing his hands across his face, he tried to erase the image of Sylvie lying in a coffin from his brain. It made no difference. He figured that image was burned into his soul forever.

She reached out and took his hand with her left one, leaving the right one free to sign. "Want to tell me about it?"

No, no.

But he stopped. Actually, he did. The words he'd kept in for so long were ready to burst from him. But only to her.

"Did my grandmother tell you that Sylvie was my stepsister?" He waited. She bobbed her fist quickly, up and down. *Yes.* "When I was a kid, my mom never had time for me. Or my dad. She was a former model, used to living well and being the center of attention. Being stuck in small-town Pennsylvania didn't appeal to her. When she left us to go back to that life, it broke my dad's heart. Then she was killed in a scandalous way, and the tabloid frenzy nearly killed him, too. My grandparents took me in, because he wasn't capable of caring for me."

Once he got started, the words erupted from him, like lava from a volcano. They burned. She didn't interrupt. And her presence was an anchor, helping him continue.

"After several years, he managed to stop drinking. And he married again. Louise, his new wife, was great. I loved her more than the mother I barely remembered. Isn't that terrible?"

Her head moved back and forth. No. But she didn't say anything, even when a tear slipped down her cheek.

"She had a daughter. Sylvie. Several years younger than me. I adored that kid. She was such a brat at times, but she was my sister, even though we weren't related by blood."

He paced to the bookshelf, looked at the pictures. The hardest part was yet to come. "My mom, though, she'd destroyed my dad's ability to trust. Louise tried to help him heal, but she eventually divorced him because she couldn't deal with the constant badgering. The lack of trust. I tried to keep in touch. And I saw Sylvie as much as I could. Then she got murdered while she was in college. And I thought I knew who did it. The woman who was convicted was released after four years. I made her life miserable. Because I knew her presence in town, walking around free after killing Sylvie, hurt Louise. You want to know the worst thing?"

He laughed. There was no humor in it.

"Turned out the woman convicted wasn't the murderer. She was innocent. My cruel, dangerous actions seriously upset a woman who had done nothing wrong. They almost cost me my job. And my self-respect. They did cost me my rank as sergeant. I decided then and there I would prove myself. Get my rank back. Which means I can't ever let my emotions get the better of me. Not again."

TWELVE

And there it was.

Dawn was breaking, and Rebecca was still tossing and turning in her bed in the guest room, unable to stop reliving the conversation she'd had with Miles several hours ago. She'd left the kitchen struggling not to show just how shattered his revelation had left her. And not just the matter of his stepsister's murder. Or his stepping out of his role as a protector and admitting his mistakes in the past. Because she knew God was merciful, and redemption was possible. Hadn't she seen for herself what an honorable man he was?

Rebecca had been telling herself from the moment she'd met him that the attraction she felt for the sincere police officer was useless. Her past had left her damaged, and with unsightly scars. When Miles had seen her scars and not been repulsed, she had allowed herself to believe that maybe, just maybe, there was hope.

But he was a police officer. A man who would always put himself in danger to help others. She had gone back and forth with herself over whether or not she could deal with his choice of career. Because it was obvious to her that being a policeman was his God-given calling. Which was something she could never challenge.

Now, it seemed, she wasn't going to have a chance to decide if she could accept it. He had told her point-blank that he didn't do relationships. Which meant that he, too, had experienced attraction on some level. Experienced it and decided against it.

How dare he make that decision for both of them? The heat of the blush on her face wasn't just caused by anger. She remembered the way she had embraced him when he'd come in. The warmth of his arms had made her feel so safe. Cared for. Had she imagined it?

No! He'd hugged her back, just as fiercely. But he insisted on acting like it didn't matter.

Well, she definitely wasn't going to be able to sleep. Swinging her legs over the side of the bed, she slid forward until her feet touched the wooden floor. And immediately snatched them up again. It had been a long time since she'd set her bare feet on cold wooden floors. Not since she'd left home. Her parents' plain house didn't have a single inch of carpeting in it. Her *mam* and *dat* believed that was too fancy. She was used to that once, but had long since developed a liking for warm, soft rugs protecting her feet from cold floors first thing in the morning.

Feeling foolish for letting such a silly thing stop her, she slapped her feet down again and ignored the discomfort. But only until she'd snagged a clean pair of socks from her bag.

Next, she grabbed her laptop. Hurrying back to the bed, she booted it up and logged on to the *Erie Times News*. Nothing interesting on the front page of the paper's website. It was all election news. People were still in shock that Seth's dad was retiring from his job as a senator. The opponents for the open seat were vicious in their attacks of each other.

Bored, she logged on to her Facebook account and started to scroll down the news feed. After a few minutes, she stopped. Stared.

Time stood still. For a few moments, she couldn't take it in. There had to be a mistake.

But there it was in full color. Brooke's picture. She was smiling and carefree. Someone had posted an article. *Local Missionary Vanishes Upon Return*.

A sick churning started in her stomach as she read the story carefully. Brooke had returned from her mission trip. There were witnesses that she had been picked up from the airport by her mother. For the next day, her parents had organized a welcome-home party for her. She never showed up.

But the connection had been made. The article went into detail about the abduction from years earlier, and the fate and whereabouts of each of the other girls today.

Horrified, she started to read the comments. Some were sympathetic, some not so much. And one made her blood turn to ice.

Someone had written "I hope the last girl is ok. I saw her. She was dropped off at my neighbor's house. They're deaf, too."

How hard would it be to find out where the woman lived and who was deaf on her street?

She couldn't stay here! Miles's uncle and grandparents weren't safe with her around!

Without conscious thought, she grabbed the laptop and flew through the empty hallway and down the stairs. She tripped on the last stair. Pain seared through her foot as her big toe was bent back. She didn't even slow down.

Miles was asleep on the couch, his arm flung over his eyes as he slept.

Halting beside the couch, she yelled out.

Miles jackknifed up off the couch, his eyes wild. His left hand was at his waist, about where his gun usually was. He sank back down when he saw her, his head falling to lean against the back of the couch. She could see his chest rise as he drew in a deep breath.

"Rebecca." His greeting was remarkably calm, considering she'd just terrified him. "Is something wrong?"

Instead of answering, she thrust the open computer into his arms. The screen was blank, so she toggled the mouse button to bring the article back up.

She pointed at the post, then yanked her arm back when her finger trembled. Even as she watched, another comment popped up.

Miles reached out and grabbed her hand before she could tuck it behind her back. He pulled her down to sit beside him, looping his arm around her shoulders, and hauled her closer so she was snuggled up against his side. She dropped her head on his shoulder, drained. He set the computer on the coffee table in front of him.

He was just comforting her, she reminded herself. She shouldn't read anything into this. Yet she couldn't stop herself from snuggling just a little closer. Nor did she complain when his arm squeezed her shoulders briefly in response.

He scoured the post, never removing his protective hold from her. She didn't complain, but angled her head up so she could see his face. The hair that always seemed to need a haircut was once again flopped on his forehead. In contrast, the rest of face had tightened. As his gaze skimmed down the post to read the growing list of comments, she could feel the clasp around her shoulder grow taut. In fact, Miles practically vibrated with tension.

She finally had to protest as his grip around her shoulders became unbearable. Shifting in his hold, she brought his attention back to her.

His arm loosened, although it didn't move away completely. His mouth softened. "Sorry. I didn't mean to squeeze so hard," he signed one-handed.

Her chest tightened when his gaze roamed her face, then landed on her lips. Her breathing hitched. Could he hear her heartbeat race? The hard *thud, thud* of her pulse vibrated in her throat.

"I don't think I need to tell you that this isn't a safe place for you anymore," he signed.

"I know. But what about your grandparents? Your uncle? If the killer thinks I'm staying here, they'll still be at risk, even if I leave." She would never forgive herself if something happened to these kind people because of their generosity to her.

"I am going to encourage them to go stay

with friends for a few days. Not that I think they're in trouble. So far no one has been hurt if you weren't around." She winced at that. Ouch. "I think our man's too smart for that. After all, he's avoided being caught up to now."

"Where will I go?"

It broke her heart, but she knew he'd probably put her in some safe place far away. Which meant her brother would get married without her being there. And, she jolted at the thought, she'd be left in someone else's care, away from Miles.

She wasn't ready to part with him. The emotional twang she experienced was almost a physical pain. She might never be ready to part with him. Policeman or not.

She braced herself.

Man, she was getting tense. Miles thought she'd break apart if she grew any stiffer.

"You're going to stay with me." Her posture drooped. Had she been worried he'd push her off onto someone else? Even if he'd wanted to, which he didn't, he knew the department was stretched to its full capacity right now. The chief was planning on hiring two new officers, but had not been able to yet. So until further notice, he was on Rebecca detail.

The fact that he wanted to smile at the thought

worried him, but he pushed it aside. Right now, she was only one step away from being captured and killed.

He prayed urgently that it wasn't too late for Brooke.

"I need to talk with Brooke's family again, and I can't leave you here. We'll go as soon as you are packed and we eat. And I need to talk with my family."

An hour later, she was packed and ready to go. Miles had talked with his grandparents and uncle and explained the situation. Gran was unruffled, and entirely unwilling to impose on any of their friends. When he'd tried to convince her, she'd simply shrugged, then signed, "The Lord will protect us. He always has."

Miles scratched his head. The urge to kick something was very strong. Until he saw Rebecca smile, her face soft and amused.

"What's so funny?" he signed, curiosity getting the better of him.

"Your grandmother. She reminds me of my *mam*." She signed *mother*. He automatically translated it to *mam* in his head, remembering her explanation of the Amish word for *mother*. "*Mam* and *Dat* never let anything shake their trust in God."

"Would your parents let you convince them

to move to a safe house?" he asked, his signs sharper than intended.

"No. They would not. They would consider this all part of the fancy world, and wouldn't let it bother them."

Great. Now his girl was encouraging them.

His girl? No way did he just think that. But he did.

His uncle surprised them. "I texted my brother. He is going to let us stay with him for as long we need to."

His jaw dropped. He couldn't help it. "What? My dad is letting you stay with him?"

His dad was a bit of a recluse. He didn't appreciate others in his private space. Even when Miles visited him, he was tolerated for only a day before his dad started making hints that it was time for him to leave.

"I can be persuasive when I need to be," his uncle signed back, a satisfied smirk settling over his features.

They couldn't afford to waste more time on idle chitchat. Miles hugged his family and then signed to Rebecca that it was time to go. It was just past eight fifteen when they finally hit the road.

Just in time to hit rush hour, he fumed an hour later.

Still, they managed to arrive at Brooke's parents' house by ten. Brooke's teenage brother answered the door, the pale cast to his skin proof of the horror the family was living through. Poor kid. No one should have to deal with this sort of anguish. No one.

The family wasn't alone. A woman in her forties with graying red hair sat next to Brooke's mother on the sofa, an arm around the weeping woman, and standing off to the side…

"That's April! My boss!" Rebecca signed.

April's face went ashen as she saw Miles in his police uniform. "Have they found her?" she gasped out, clearly expecting the worst.

All talking ceased. Brooke's parents, two brothers and both women focused on Miles. His heart broke a little for the mother, who was staring at him, hope and dread fighting for dominance on her face. He hoped he never had to give her the information she feared, his stepmother's ravaged expression in his mind.

He sent Rebecca an apologetic glance. She nodded. He had told her in the car that he wouldn't be able to sign to her. Technically, she shouldn't even be in the room.

"No, Mrs. Cole. I have no new information. We are still searching for your daughter. I hate to bother you at this difficult time. But I may have a lead that is connected to Brooke's disappearance. If I might have a few minutes of your time?"

"Officer, anything you need to help us get our daughter back, just name it," Brooke's father said. Harold Cole. That was his name. And his wife was Susan.

When invited, Miles sat on the empty chair near the window, ignoring the dog hairs that were sure to stick like glue to his spotless uniform. He was aware of Rebecca remaining out of the way in the doorway. Brooke's parents looked her way, but didn't say anything about her.

"When I talked with you several days ago, you never mentioned Brooke was coming home."

"We didn't know," Susan Cole replied. "She called us to say there was some sort of unrest where she was, and she was being sent home. She called us from her layover at Cleveland. We barely had time to get her."

"Do you have any idea who could be responsible?" Harold asked.

"Yes, sir. We have reason to believe Terry Gleason had a half brother he was separated from when they were children—a man who might want revenge in his brother's honor. Have you noticed any strange men around lately?"

He could tell they were trying their best to

think of anything that could help, but no one seemed to have noticed anything. After a few minutes, he concluded that there didn't seem to be anything new to be gained.

Before he left, he turned to April. "Miss Long?"

She startled. "Yes, officer?"

"I know that Rebecca works for you. May I ask how you are related to the family here?"

April didn't answer. The woman on the couch did. She looked like April. "Susan and I are stepsisters. Brooke and April are cousins."

His former suspicions regarding April returned. It was too much of a coincidence that she knew two of the victims. He wondered if she had anything else to hide. It wasn't something he wanted to get into now, not in front of the devastated family, but he intended to talk with her.

A few minutes later, he rose from his seat. "Mr. Cole. Mrs. Cole. Thank you for your time today. I give you my word that I will do everything possible to get your daughter back to you." *Hopefully, alive.* No need to say that part aloud. Nor did he deem it necessary to admit that he had a personal reason for wanting to catch this fellow immediately. Or that his personal reason was the beautiful blonde standing in the doorway, waiting for him.

He followed her back to his car, his hand

on her shoulder as his gaze darted around the street in a continuous sweep. Arriving at the car, he opened the passenger-side door and waited while she stepped into the car.

Nearby, he heard an engine rev. An orange car sped around the corner. Miles pushed Rebecca's head down. The car approached. A gun was in the driver's hand. Miles had his gun out and was aiming for the tires.

Without warning, the driver dropped his arm and sped away.

What? Why hadn't he shot?

Miles caught the first four characters of the license plate. Punching the button on his radio, he reported the details to the dispatcher. He also was able to tell her the make and model of the car. "The driver is armed and dangerous."

It shouldn't take them that long to identify the plate, if it belonged to that car.

"Who was that? Was he holding a gun?"

Miles spun around. April was standing five feet away, her face drawn and ashen. Did she think she was going to get hurt? Or did she have another reason for being so upset?

Whatever her reason was, he now thought he knew what had sent the driver racing away without finishing his quest. Given his prior behavior, Miles would have expected the man to kill him and take Rebecca. Although if she had died, the perp probably wouldn't have cared. Miles figured that he was expendable because he was obviously searching for the attacker's identity.

Well, he wasn't going to stop now. He would keep searching, looking under every possible rock, in order to protect Rebecca. And if he ended up getting hurt saving her, it would be worth it.

His radio crackled back to life. "Officer Olsen? We have the make and model of the car. It is registered to a Nicole Weller."

Nicole Weller. Looks like he'd just found his next rock to overturn.

"Great job. Where is this Nicole Weller located?"

THIRTEEN

You know something's wrong when you see an Amish man at the police station.

Miles took a swig of Mountain Dew and screwed the cap back on without taking his eyes off the man. Levi Miller—Rebecca's brother. He remembered him well. It had only been four months since Miles had last seen him. He still remembered Levi's petrified expression as he had sat beside Rebecca while she drove. Well, to be fair, she was driving very fast at the time.

What was he doing at the station? The Amish community didn't go seeking outside help. Unless it was an emergency.

Levi saw him and made a beeline for Miles's desk. Miles raised his eyebrows before he managed to hide his response. One of these days he'd learn to control his features. It was just natural to let his face and body language speak for him. That's what happened when one was partially raised by deaf grandparents.

"Officer Olsen." The Amish man halted in front of his desk.

"Mr. Miller. How can I help you?"

"My sister Rebecca is missing."

"Missing?" Oh, wait. He'd never even thought of the fact that there would be no phone at the Miller home, no way to send them a message to let them know she was all right, short of going there to tell them in person. "She's not missing. She's here at the moment."

Levi let out a loud sigh. Miles knew relief when he heard it, and felt his own guilt grow in response. He should have contacted them to let them know they didn't need to be worried about her. "That is *gut*. I was worried about her. She hasn't contacted the family since Wednesday. I went over to see her at her apartment. She wasn't there. I went to where she works, and the store was closed. Not even Jess could tell me where she was. Only that she was fine, and I needed to come and see you."

Miles smiled at the man. The family might have trouble communicating with her sometimes, but it was very clear that they loved her dearly.

"She's here, in the conference room. I'll take you to her." Miles tossed down the pen he'd been fiddling with and stood, indicating that Levi should come with him. "I moved her to a safe location. Until the situation is under control, I don't want her to be alone." As concisely as possible, Miles explained what had happened over the past several days.

"She is all right, *jah*?" Levi asked when he was finished. "She was not seriously hurt?"

"She's fine." He hastened to reassure the man. "A little shook up, and I'd say impatient to get back to her normal schedule, but I'm doing all I can to find the guy responsible and keep her safe. We all are."

"That is *gut*," the Amish man said simply, his calm demeanor firmly back in place.

This was his chance, Miles realized. He rubbed the back of his neck, grimacing as he realized how warm it was. Great. He probably looked like a blond lobster. But he couldn't waste the opportunity. He looked across at the other man. Levi was scrutinizing him. Yep. His nerves were showing.

Get it over with.

Clearing his throat, he plunged in. "Mr. Miller, Rebecca is determined to go to your wedding on Thursday."

The man's face fell. "It is too dangerous?"

Aw, man. "No. I mean, there are precautions we can take so she can still be there. She was going to ask if I could go with her. Just to keep watch over her, and get her out of there if it seemed necessary. I hope nothing will happen, but I don't want to take a chance."

Why did he feel like a teenager asking a father if he could date his daughter? This was police business. He was doing his job. That was all. Except, it was Rebecca. And he'd never thought of any of the other people he'd helped in the same light as he did her.

Levi was thinking, bobbing his head. "*Jah.* That could work. If you protect my little sister." Here the man cast as stern a glance as any father ever had at the police officer. As if he knew Miles was developing stronger feelings for his sister. Which could be awkward.

It was a relief to finally reach the conference room. He swung open the door, then stepped back to let Levi precede him into the room. Rebecca was flipping through one of the books she'd stuffed in her backpack.

Miles rapped on the table and Rebecca looked up. Then, beaming, she launched herself into her brother's arms. Levi returned her embrace, although he seemed a little uncomfortable. Probably wasn't used to being demonstrative.

"What are you doing here? I wasn't expecting to see you before the wedding!" she signed. She repeated her signs, slower, when Levi didn't understand her the first time around.

"I was worried about you. I went to your

apartment this morning. The door was open, so I went in." The man hesitated.

A wordless whimper escaped Rebecca's throat.

Levi made a calming gesture. "I didn't see anything broken. Drawers and cupboards open." He made a final sign, giving his hands one quick shake. "That's all."

What? Why hadn't he said something earlier about the break-in? Instead, they'd talked about his wedding.

Miles said as much to him.

The Amish man swallowed. "It is not easy for me to come to the police with my troubles, to report crimes like break-ins and robbery. When I came to see you, my worry was for my sister's safety. I did not care about the break-in, I only wanted to know she was safe."

Rebecca backed up and shook her head, face ashen. Was she going to pass out? Miles took three quick steps to her side. She slumped back into her chair before he could touch her. He settled a hand on her shoulder, gave a gentle squeeze.

"I'm here," he signed when her eyes met his. "I promise I won't let anything happen to you."

"Someone was in my apartment, going through my things. How long can this continue?"

He couldn't ignore her distress. Nor could he follow his instincts and pull her into his arms. Not while standing in the police station in full uniform. And definitely not in front of her older brother. Especially knowing how strict the Amish community was about public displays of affection except between family members. He'd done some research once he knew there was a possibility that he'd be traveling into Amish territory for the wedding. It was pretty much what he'd expected. Except that the bride and groom would not kiss.

The unbidden image of Rebecca's face close enough to his to kiss blindsided him. He blinked. Shook his head. Can't go there.

Rebecca and Levi were both watching him. Great.

He remembered Rebecca's fear. That, he could deal with. "I think the person was just trying to find where you went. Now that the story about you being at my grandparents' house has broken, we can't go back there. But the chief told me an hour ago that Parker is out of the hospital. And the emergency at the center is about over. So we will have the manpower to protect you and anyone else involved wherever you decide to stay."

He brushed a strand of hair from her face. Her gaze found his and stayed.

The phone rang, breaking the spell.

Backing away from her, he answered the phone. "Officer Olsen."

"Olsen," the chief said, his normal drawl a terse bark. Miles instinctively straightened and threw back his shoulders. That tone of voice never boded well. "Your DNA from the bubble gum at the crime scene came back. It belongs to a young man named Chad Weller. Details and a picture are being faxed to you right now."

"Weller? The license plates and car I reported today were licensed to a Nicole Weller."

"His ex-wife. He has a record of domestic abuse, but charges were always dropped before he could be brought to trial."

"Figures. Did he steal the car? And if he did, could the ex-wife be convinced to testify against him?"

"That's what I need you to find out."

"I'm on it."

He hung up the phone and turned to find Rebecca and Levi watching him. "That was the chief." He related the pertinent details.

"You could maybe find this man now, *jah*?"

Miles sighed, rubbing his neck. He could really use a Mountain Dew right about now. "Maybe, but I don't think it will be easy."

"I can bring Rebecca home with me. Then she could just stay for the wedding. That would be *gut*."

Uh, no, it wouldn't. He might like Levi and all, but to trust him to take Rebecca forty-five minutes away in an unprotected buggy? Yeah, not happening.

"I think I will bring her with me. I will bring her to your house tomorrow night before the wedding and we'll both plan to stay. How about that?"

Miles could tell Levi wasn't happy about it, but he didn't argue. Neither did Rebecca, which surprised him. He'd expected her to want to go and stay with her family right away. That's what she had originally wanted. But that was before she was shot at and so ruthlessly targeted. He imagined she was worried about putting her family in danger with her presence.

Lord, I don't want to fail this woman. Please guide me. Help me to protect her.

It was almost four in the afternoon when Miles parked the cruiser in the driveway of the house belonging to Nicole Weller. Rebecca sat quietly, apparently lost in her own thoughts. He frowned. Something felt off. He couldn't quite put his finger on it.

Then he realized the house looked abandoned. The full garbage can was still up near the garage. The other houses on the street had their cans near the curb, empty. It seemed to be garbage day, but she hadn't brought hers down. From where he sat, he could see at least three newspapers in the paper box at the side of the road. If he had a warrant to look, he'd probably find several days' worth of mail in the box.

"I don't like this," he signed. "Stay close, and do whatever I tell you without asking questions."

"I will."

They went up the three steps to the house. His hand slid to his waist and he removed his gun. Better to be safe.

Nerves jangling, he rang the doorbell. No answer. Leaning to the side, he peered into a dark window. Was that movement?

"Mrs. Weller, LaMar Pond Police Department. Do you need assistance?"

A muffled crash. Followed by a low groan. Someone was in pain.

"Mrs. Weller, I'm coming in."

The door was unlocked. Shoving it open, he went in first, gun ready as he checked every direction for danger. Seeing none, he continued in, aware of Rebecca behind him. Nicole Weller was lying on the floor in her own blood. She was alive. Badly beaten. But alive.

A quick prayer of thanksgiving. He used his shoulder radio to call 911. Then he kneeled by her side. Her lashes fluttered.

"Mrs. Weller, can you hear me?" A groan answered him. "Mrs. Weller, can you tell me who did this to you?"

He knew, but he needed confirmation.

She sucked in a shallow raspy breath. When she spoke, he leaned closer so he could hear her. "Chad…so angry…tried to kill me."

In the silence that descended the harsh breathing of the injured woman was amplified. He closed his eyes as a wave of gratitude surged through his veins. This could have been Rebecca. But it wasn't. And if he had his way, neither Rebecca, nor Nicole Weller, nor any other woman, would die at the hands of Chad Weller ever again.

The image of the injured woman stayed with Rebecca for the remainder of the day. She had returned to the Travis house, and as Miles had said, Parker was there to guard her. He seemed embarrassed at having failed her before, and was doubly determined to protect Rebecca at every moment.

By Wednesday morning, she was ready to climb the walls.

Miles was busy making sure Ashley and Nicole were both safe. It was both good and bad that they were in cities run by different departments, he'd explained to her. Good because

LaMar Pond was a small-town force, and didn't have the manpower to protect all those different women around the clock at the same time. But also bad, because it meant that they were more difficult to keep track of.

Finally, it was time to go to her family's house. Normally, she would have enjoyed the trip. This time she couldn't. As she got into Miles's car, the hair on the back of her neck stood on end.

"What's wrong?" he signed.

"I keep waiting for someone to jump out at us with a gun."

He nodded. "I'm going to take a roundabout way to make us harder to follow. And I have alerted the local police in that area of the issue, plus sent them what we have on Weller. Which isn't much. If he got into any trouble in high school, those files are sealed. There's nothing from the time he turned eighteen until he married Nicole and she filed domestic abuse charges. He kept to himself. His last known address was near Cleveland. At present, no one seems to know where he is."

It seemed like he had thought of everything. But she still couldn't shake the feeling dogging her that something bad was coming their way.

They made it to her parents' house without any mishaps. She should have been relieved.

The large white farmhouse was bursting with joy and activity as her parents and her five siblings worked. And yet the ache in her stomach wouldn't go away. She had to keep reminding herself to unwrap her arms from around her waist. When her mother asked her if she was fine in her halting sign language, Rebecca forced herself to paste a smile on her face and nod. *Mam* frowned, but let it go.

Soon, the entire family was involved in wedding preparations. Most of the cooking would happen the next morning. But her family still had much to do to get ready for all the guests that would soon descend on them. Rebecca found herself doing whatever jobs she could that required very little communication.

At one point, Levi asked Miles if he could help moving benches. She could tell he was going to refuse so he could stay near her.

"I'm fine," she signed to him. "I will be in here, with my family."

He didn't look convinced, but finally agreed.

Every few minutes, she'd go to the window to search for a mop of floppy blond hair. Once, she looked out and saw him standing with Levi, laughing. He glanced up and caught her eyes. The laughter stopped. Immediately, he signed, "Are you all right?"

She nodded. "Just checking." Her cheeks

grew warm. Now he'd know how much she was relying on him. Knowing how he avoided emotional attachments, she wasn't anxious to see his reaction. He surprised her, though. A warm glance caressed her face. Her face grew even warmer, although not with trepidation. "I won't leave," he signed. "I promise."

She nodded, then returned her focus to the room. Her sister Lizzy watched her, brows raised high. Great. Lizzy could never stand to be kept out of any secret. Her little sister was only sixteen, but looked so much more mature. Actually, now that she thought about it, Lizzy looked exactly like Rebecca had several years before.

"What are you working on?" her sister signed to her.

She looked over to where she had been doing some mending and noticed that her aunt had stepped in and taken it over.

"Nothing."

Lizzy's eyes lit up immediately. "Perfect! You can come with me. I need to take the buggy to Aunt Lavinia's to pick up some things. We haven't had time alone together in so long."

Rebecca bit her lip. The urge to go with her sister was strong. But for the two of them to go off alone, well, that wouldn't be smart.

Some of what she was feeling must have

shown on her face. Lizzy sidled over to her gave her a pleading look, her sister's blue eyes huge. She even batted her lashes for good measure. Rebecca held a hand over her mouth to cover lips that quivered with the urge to smile.

"Please? You can dress in one of your old dresses and *kapps*. The person after you has never seen you in Amish dress. I doubt he knows where you're from. And we are only going a mile away from here. We should be back in less than thirty minutes."

It would be nice to get away from the fear for a bit. And Lizzy was right. Chad Weller had never seen her in her Amish attire. Even his brother hadn't—she'd been in Englisch clothes when she'd gone out that night with Holly and her friends.

Holly. A hollow pang hit her in the chest.

Unable to stand thinking about her dead friend, she nodded to her sister. "Just let me go change." She ran up to her old room and found one of her old dresses and a *kapp*.

"Are you ready?" Lizzy signed when she tripped back down the stairs.

Reluctantly, she nodded. But her heart was heavy.

Outside, she peered around for Miles. She could let him know where she was going. But she couldn't spot him, and her sister was grabbing her arm and pulling.

"Come on. I told Ruth to tell your friend where we were going."

Good. Their youngest sister could be trusted to do what Lizzy told her to.

They hitched up the horse to the buggy. "I want to drive," Lizzy signed. Naturally. It had been so long since Rebecca had driven one, she preferred that her sister take charge of the vehicle.

The hairs on the back of her neck stood on end. Was someone watching her? Moving her head from side to side, she tried to see if anyone stood out. She didn't even try to act nonchalant. What was the point? But she saw nothing suspicious. She was letting her fears get the better of her.

Still, she clambered up into the buggy quickly.

Lizzy climbed up beside her and gathered the reins in her hands. It was almost all Rebecca could do to keep from yanking the reins from her sister and making the single horse move faster. Not that they would be able to pick up any speed until they reached the paved road at the intersection. Suddenly, the half hour her sister had quoted seemed like a very long time.

They arrived at the intersection without incident. The road was clear, so her sister moved the buggy out onto the paved road. That was when a car roared up behind them. It pulled into the left lane, as if to pass, then slowed to keep pace with them. Lizzy threw an irritated glance over her shoulder, then the color drained from her face. Rebecca followed her line of vision. The white car beside them was nothing out of the ordinary. Rebecca had never seen it before. But she had seen the man in the ski mask behind the wheel. She screamed as she saw the rifle being held in one hand. Pointing right at them.

Rebecca reached out and jerked on the reins. The horse, startled, reared. Lizzy let go of the reins and covered her face, letting her older sister take control. Rebecca steered the buggy into the yard beside them. The car moved as if to slam into them.

A semitruck crested the hill, heading toward them. The car shot ahead.

The semi flew past.

The brief feeling of respite ended as the car slammed on its brakes. A second car passed them and slowed, giving them a buffer. But a very small one. They only had a moment before the driver could reach them.

Rebecca didn't even bother signing. She clutched her sister's sleeve and literally yanked her out of the buggy. Chances of outrunning the

man were slim, but they would give it their best
try. Giving up was not an option.

Oh, why hadn't she told Miles where they
were going?

You didn't want him to tell you not to go.
It was true. She had allowed her desire for a
peaceful interlude with her sister to overcome
her common sense.

Out of the corner of her eye, she saw the car
door open, and a figure in black charged from
the car. She froze briefly, terror taking hold.
Only for a second. Then she grabbed her sister's sweaty hand and hauled her as fast as she
could toward the woods.

A chunk of dirt flying up a foot in front of
her made her stumble. He was shooting at them!
She righted herself and flashed her eyes to her
sister. Please…oh, please, let her be okay.

She was. Terrified, but uninjured.

Rebecca sent up a prayer to keep it that way.

A tug on her hand pulled her to a stop. What
was Lizzy thinking? Some madman was trying
to kill them. They needed to run.

She tried to pull her sister with her, but Lizzy
dug in her heels and yanked on Rebecca's hand
until she was forced to turn. That's when she
noticed the blue and red flashing strobe lights
reflecting on the trees.

She nearly fainted from relief. Hot tears

burned in her eyes. She didn't even try to hold back the sobs. Miles had arrived. And the man shooting at them was speeding away. Blinking, she saw that the blond cop was holding his watch up to his mouth and talking fast, even as he charged toward them. Most likely telling the police where he was and what had happened.

He took a small leap to bridge the shallow ditch and reach the girls. She launched herself at him and found herself caught up against his chest. Burying her face in his neck, she continued to shake and cry. Eventually, she became aware that he was rubbing her back in soothing circles with unsteady hands. Every few seconds, she felt him kiss her hair.

Lifting her face, she blinked away the remainder of her tears. She needed to tell him they were fine. And to apologize for her poor judgment, which could have ended disastrously.

She never got the chance. He kissed her the moment she looked up. The feel of his lips touching hers made everything else fade.

The sweet kiss ended. He lifted his face away from hers, searched her face and then kissed her a second time. Her fists held on to his shirt as she breathed in his clean sent.

Lizzy! She'd totally forgotten her sister. Breaking away, she blushed as she cut her eyes to her sister. Lizzy rolled her eyes and grinned. Shyly, Rebecca looked through her lashes at Miles.

"Are you two hurt?" he signed. When they shook their heads, he sighed and gave Rebecca another quick hug.

"Aren't you going to lecture us?" Rebecca asked, wrinkling her nose.

He quirked a grin. "You know it. When you are safely inside the house again. Never do that to me again. Promise?"

For the first time, she noticed the shadow in his eyes. His sister had been murdered, she remembered. And here she was putting herself in danger when she knew he felt responsible for her safety. She couldn't believe how selfish she had been. Moving up on her tiptoes, she kissed him softly. A kiss of apology.

"I promise. I won't put you through that again."

He ran his fingers down her cheek. "Let's go. I have the local police searching for the car. But let's not take any chances. I have a feeling that he won't give up until we stop him."

Or until he finishes what he started, she thought.

FOURTEEN

The morning of the wedding dawned clear, although there was a definite nip in the air. Miles finished dressing for the day and went to find Rebecca. He'd tossed and turned late into the night, the image of Rebecca dragging her sister across the field while being shot at seared into his brain.

Whether he was aware of it before or not, the killer now knew that Rebecca had Amish roots. And that she was in town for a wedding.

Jackson had called later to let him know that the car had been found, abandoned. As expected, it had been a stolen vehicle. Jackson would be arriving soon, as would Parker. When informed of the almost tragic incident less than a mile away, Mr. Miller had agreed to allow Miles to put extra security precautions in place. Which included more police at the house during the reception.

The problem was that the actual ceremony

wouldn't be at the Millers' house. Miles had wanted to pull his hair out when he'd learned this little tidbit. Apparently, weddings were so much work, that the wedding often happened at a relative's house. In this case, Mr. Miller's brother was hosting the wedding. So all the benches they had loaded onto the tractor last night were set up at the uncle's house.

Jackson and Parker would be relegated to strolling the perimeter of the property. Which was fine. Miles would be at the wedding itself. They could keep the threat at bay from the outside. The officers would not be in uniform so as not to distress the guests or disturb the ceremony, but all Miles cared about was that they would be there and he would be able to protect his Rebecca.

He stopped. His Rebecca. How he wished it was true. The kisses last night had come from the strong emotions arising from seeing her in danger. Yet he couldn't help thinking they would have happened sooner or later.

He needed to focus on keeping her safe. Maybe later, after all the danger had passed, he could figure out a way to meld his career and his personal desires. He refused to consider that maybe he would fail to keep her safe. But the fear lurked in shadows, and it wore Sylvie's face, reminding him that he had failed once before.

Enough! He had a wedding to attend and a woman to protect.

He had decided to wear his gun after all. It was well disguised under his jacket, so none of the guests needed to even know of its presence.

Clomping down to the kitchen, he paused at the doorway. And forgot to breathe.

Rebecca was already there at the table. She wasn't dressed plain. Instead, she was wearing a simple A-line dress of cobalt blue. Her shoulder-length golden blond hair was swept up into a simple bun at the back of her head and held in place by some sort of clip.

She took his breath away.

One of her brothers asked him a question. Which one was it? He knew her two brothers were Thomas and Joseph, both in their late teens. Problem was, they looked like twins. He answered the questions and watched as the morning wore on and guests arrived. He was pleased to note that Seth and Jess were there, not just because he liked the couple immensely, but also because he was glad that Rebecca would have other proficient signers around to keep her company. He really liked her family. They were down-to-earth, kind, generous people. But it grieved him to think of Rebecca growing up with communication barriers putting distance between her and her loved ones. Having never been to an Amish wedding, he was amazed at the magnitude of the event. Almost three hundred people were there. In a barn. The benches he had helped the men to move the night before were facing each other. The men sat on one side and the women on the other.

As a non-Amish guest, he sat outside the barn on metal bleachers with Rebecca, Seth, Jess and the few other Englischers who were at the wedding. He had pulled the metal bleacher in as close to the barn as possible. And had gained permission to put it under a tent. That way they wouldn't be sitting there with invisible targets on their backs. Still, he was unable to relax and enjoy the wedding. Even knowing that Parker and Jackson were both on duty, making rounds and keeping track of everything going on around them, his teeth were on edge. Every thirty seconds or so, he let his gaze drift to the trees and the outskirts of the property. The one negative thing about the tent was that even though it limited the killer's view of them, Miles's vision was also cut off.

Was that a movement? Near the north end? He couldn't be sure, but he wouldn't relax until he knew. As discreetly as possible, he tapped out a text to the two cops roaming the grounds. Then he tapped his fingers anxiously on his knee while he waited, his body tense and ready to move. Another movement in that area and he would grab Rebecca and…

A warm hand smoothed over on top of his. Rebecca. He drew in a deep breath.

His watch vibrated. Finally. Jackson. He had scoured the area that Miles had indicated. There were footprints. But they were much too small to have belonged to Weller.

That was a small relief. But he didn't let his guard down. He was convinced that Weller was escalating his attacks. They were getting closer and deadlier, as if the man had realized he had to work fast to achieve his goal. Miles shuddered. His goal was to eliminate the woman Miles lov—

No.

Yes. He briefly closed his eyes. Everything he had done to stay unattached had failed. His heart belonged to the slender woman seated so peacefully at his side. He opened his eyes, and they immediately slid to Rebecca. And found her gaze on him, questioning, her forehead wrinkled in concern.

The urge to run his hand over those lines and smooth them out did nothing to lessen his inner anguish. He couldn't let himself give in to emotion. Not when his future, and hers, depended on it.

But would he be able to walk away from her

when the case was over? And say he did manage to walk away...

The pain that hit him stole his breath. He rubbed a hand over his chest. He was in deep. And he wasn't sure if there was anything he could do to change it.

By the time the ceremony ended, he had a roaring headache. And a stiff neck. No doubt from the constant strain of watching in all directions for a threat to emerge. The guests emerged from the barn and started to walk toward the road. The reception would be held at the Millers' house. Fortunately, that was only two houses down the road.

How long would they have to stay? He was anxious to get Rebecca back to where he was more familiar with the layout. And where there weren't so many people around. It was almost noon. Rebecca had said the reception could last for a few hours, but should break up by midafternoon.

As they walked, a car drove up beside them. Miles moved quickly, putting himself on the outside and Rebecca closer to the edge of the road. His hand moved to his gun. The car pulled up beside them. A young man in a baseball cap. Too young to be Weller. He relaxed. The car continued on ahead of them, turning at the intersection.

They arrived at the Miller house. He had

never been so happy to see a house in his life. The yard was full of buggies, and soon the air was thick with laughter.

Miles had a brief word with Jackson and Parker about the possible threats and hiding places for an attacker, then he returned to the reception. The feast provided by the family looked fantastic. His stomach grumbled loudly, reminding him that it had been hours since breakfast. He watched Rebecca pick at her food.

An hour into the reception, Jackson came to find him. He moved outside to talk with his colleague, leaving Rebecca safe inside with her family.

"We have a problem. The dogs chained up outside? It looks like they've been drugged. They're breathing, and appear to be fine, but they won't wake up. I found Benadryl tablets mixed in with their food."

He was here. The killer was here. "Keep searching for him. He's here."

Miles made it back into the house in half the time it had taken to leave.

His heart slammed against his ribs.

Rebecca was gone.

Rebecca was getting worried. After lunch, Lizzy had left to go ask their mother something and hadn't returned. Remembering the way the driver had gone after them in the buggy yesterday, her stomach cramped, as she worried that Lizzy was in danger. Being in the Amish community was not the haven she had thought it would be. Yesterday had proven that. And the killer was getting desperate. He didn't even care that others were getting hurt. She remembered something that Jess had said when she'd arrived and seen Lizzy and Rebecca standing together.

"She looks just like you, Rebecca."

Jess had meant it as a compliment, and had smiled as she had signed it. And Rebecca had rolled her eyes and laughed.

She wasn't laughing now.

She was being targeted. And the sister that could be easily mistaken for her was outside on her own. She tried to remind herself that the whole day had gone so smoothly. And there were so many friends and relatives about. This was probably the safest place she could be.

But no arguments would calm her nerves. The trembling hands and the agitation would not stop until she knew that Lizzy was safe and sound.

She had to find her sister. She wished she could tell Miles, but when she had slipped out the front door, he was in an intense conversation on his phone. She had left a message with her brother Joseph to have Miles find her as soon as he was off the phone.

He had nodded. She watched him approach the newlyweds and sighed. She had watched Levi and Laura, and realized, more than ever, that she wanted that with the man she married someday. Their communication was visible in every look and expression.

She'd never find that in her parents' community.

That's not important now—find Lizzy. Get her back inside and out of danger.

Where had Lizzy gone?

Rebecca had been searching for her sister for almost twenty minutes. No one seemed to have seen her. Of course, there was always the possibility that they hadn't quite understood what she was asking. But she was fairly sure she'd gotten her point across. Her family might not all sign well, but they did all know the basics. Such as name signs.

Mam had shaken her head then made the sign for *barn.* So Rebecca had walked in the direction of the barn.

No Lizzy.

She'd trekked through the fields behind the barn, and into the other buildings. The silo. The second barn, where the animals were kept. She'd even walked down to the neighbor's house.

Nothing.

Finally, she headed home. Maybe Lizzy had shown up while she was away.

Wait a second. She stopped. That was Lizzy's bonnet.

Her heart ceased beating, then took off like a freight train. Beside the bonnet, the grass and dirt were scuffed up. Almost as if her sister had been struggling with someone.

Her chest clenched tight, cutting off air to her lungs. It felt like she was trying to breathe through a straw. Her baby sister was in the clutches of a madman!

Calm down. You don't know for sure what happened. But she couldn't shake the image of her sister being dragged away, the discarded bonnet a symbol of the evil that had once again entered their lives.

Without giving herself time to talk herself out of it, she followed the trail. Behind the out-building. Toward the pond.

The pond! Was the sadistic monster planning on drowning her sweet sister?

Miles. If Miles was here he'd know what to do. Oh, why hadn't she waited for him to be free to come with her? Her urgency to track down her sister may have very well cost Lizzy her life.

Rounding the corner, she gasped. Lizzy was struggling with a man in a ski mask.

He looked smaller than before. And not as strong. Because Lizzy was holding her own. Fortunately, there wasn't a gun in sight. There was a rather large stick on the ground. Perfect. Rebecca hefted it in her hands and grasped it like a baseball bat. Then, giving a yell that scratched her throat raw, she rushed the man holding her sister.

He reacted immediately, dropping the Amish girl and whirling to face this new threat, his arms out to defend himself. Rebecca plowed into him, arm swinging the branch. It connected soundly with his left side. She felt the impact all the way through her. He must have felt it, too, for he doubled over.

Rebecca became aware of others racing toward them. Miles was in the lead. Uh-oh. She'd have some explaining to do later.

But at least both she and Lizzy would be alive for it.

Miles reached them. Instead of the lecture she expected, he pulled her into his arms and squeezed. She could feel his heart racing through his shirt. Guess she wasn't the only one who was scared.

Abruptly, Miles released her and turned his police stare on the man still crouched in front of them, holding his gut. Lizzy scooted around them, giving the man a wide berth, and stood shoulder-to-shoulder with Rebecca.

She was pale. Though her eyes were furious. Rebecca placed an arm around her and directed her toward their parents. Once she was in *Mam*'s arms, Rebecca moved back to where she could see Miles. And the man who had caused her such misery.

Miles reached out and removed the ski mask. Rebecca felt as though the ground had fallen out from under her. She knew the man in front of her.

She waved her hand, getting Miles's attention. "I know him," she signed when he looked her way. "That's Wyatt. He makes deliveries to our store."

Miles's expression hardened. Suddenly the young man she often thought looked too fresh-faced to be a policeman looked every inch an officer. She shivered, and chanced another look at the miserable young man before them. He certainly didn't look like a hardened criminal. Nor could she imagine those thin arms reaching out and strangling her in her car…

That was it! She knew what was missing.

The tattoo.

"Miles…this is not the man who attacked me before," she signed frantically.

"Are you sure?" he signed back. But the look

on his face said he had already come to the same conclusion. They were still looking for Chad Weller.

"Absolutely. Remember? The man who attacked me before had a tattoo on his wrist."

Both of them looked at Wyatt's wrists. Neither of them sported a tattoo. Miles nodded. "Okay, but that doesn't explain this fellow attacking your sister." He leveled a glare at the now cringing man before them. "I need to question him. I can do it easier if I don't sign. I will share any pertinent facts later."

She nodded, understanding. Police business was different.

Reaching out, he surprised her by squeezing her hand and giving her a smile. Then he retracted his smile, and froze Wyatt with the ice in his eyes. She could see Wyatt's Adam's apple bob as he gulped.

By the time Miles was finished barking questions at him, rapid-fire, Rebecca's anger was starting to be replaced by sympathy. Wyatt seemed to be shrinking with each question that hit him.

Finally, Miles pulled a piece of paper from his pocket and showed him. It was a picture. It looked like a driver's license photo. A young man with longish black hair and a beard. Was that the picture he'd been sent of Chad? The brown eyes and bushy eyebrows were familiar. Had she met him before?

Wyatt was jabbering fast, his hands gesturing wildly at the picture.

Miles finally turned to Rebecca, disgust on his face. He switched to ASL. "He was in jail with Terry Gleason the last six months of Terry's life. Grew to admire him. Terry told him how he'd been framed by you girls. When Wyatt was released, Chad approached him. He," he pointed a finger at Wyatt, "agreed to help him get even. He drove the vehicle at your apartment. And he broke into your apartment and stole the picture. He's not very loyal. He's agreed to help the forensic artist create a more accurate image of Weller."

Rebecca understood. The killer was getting desperate. And more dangerous by the moment. They were running out of time.

FIFTEEN

They returned to LaMar Pond that afternoon in two cars. Jackson and Parker had Wyatt with them in a cruiser. Miles followed behind with Rebecca and Lizzy in his Jeep. He'd changed into his uniform, and his suit was packed away again.

He hadn't intended on having both sisters with him. In fact, he had fully expected Mr. and Mrs. Miller to refuse to allow their younger daughter to come to the station to give a statement. Mr. Miller, however, had surprised him.

"Two of my daughters have been attacked," he'd informed Miles. "These children were given to me by *Got* to protect and raise. I will let her make a statement so I can do *Got*'s will and protect them."

So, the teenager now sat calmly in his back seat. Although, he suspected neither of his passengers were truly calm. He'd seen Rebecca twisting her fingers. It wouldn't surprise him if Lizzy was doing the same in the back.

The small group arrived at the station and hurried inside. He had both women precede him and kept his right hand on his gun. The left he placed on Rebecca's back. Partly to keep her moving, and partly, he admitted to himself, to assure himself of her continued presence. That she was well. All the smiles from the wedding had faded.

They were dealing with a killer who was determined to kill again.

They had to wait for another forty-five minutes for the sketch artist to arrive. Miles stopped at the vending machine on the way to the conference room and got some bottles of water and a Mountain Dew. It looked like this could take a long time. He figured he would need the caffeine before the day was done.

When the sketch was finally done, Miles ordered Wyatt to be booked and then went to find the Miller girls. They were in the conference room with Jackson, who had replenished their drinks and found them some snacks. The feast at the reception had been amazing, but he knew Rebecca had been unable to eat much. And who could blame her with all she'd been through?

He came into the room and sat down beside her, touching her hand on the table briefly in the guise of getting her attention. The truth, though, was that he needed to touch her, to tell her silently that he was there. And because that small touch reassured him that she was fine.

He was a mess.

But he would do anything, put himself in front of any danger, to see that she was safe. He might not have anything else to offer her. But he could do that.

Please, Lord. You know I love her. Please help me keep her safe. Even if she isn't meant to be mine.

Right. Back to business.

He laid a picture on the table in front of her.

"This is how Chad Weller looks now. Do you recognize him?" he signed.

Rebecca gasped, her hand flying out to grab the picture and bring it closer. "I know this man!" she signed. "That's April's boyfriend!"

"April Long? Your boss?" How many Aprils could there be? But he had to be sure.

"Yes. But I don't understand. She is Brooke's cousin. Isn't that what her mother said?"

His gut twisted at the pain on her face. "Yes, that's what she said."

"Then how can she be dating the man who killed Holly? Who abducted her own cousin and may have killed her, too?" Her eyes grew damp at the last thought.

He reached out and squeezed her hand. "Let's not think about that yet. We don't know what has happened to Brooke. And we don't know the extent of April's connection."

"Do you think she knew he was waiting in my car that night?"

He shrugged, helpless. He wished he had the answers for her questions. "I have no idea. But I will get answers for you. I promise."

She stared up at him. Then the corners of her mouth lifted. It broke his heart. She was trying to be brave, while he could tell she was being torn apart.

The door flew open.

Miles and Jackson both jumped to their feet.

"Sorry, sorry!" Parker raised both hands. "I know better than to charge in like that."

Yeah, he did. Something big must have happened.

"Spit it out, Parker!"

Wow, had he just barked like that? Parker's grimace was all the answer he needed.

"Didn't mean to yell."

"No prob, Olsen. But the girl in the coma? She's awake. And she remembers everything."

"We're on our way."

It was close to six in the evening when they arrived in Cleveland. Miles hadn't taken any chances. He'd insisted on bringing Rebecca and

Lizzy along. Parker had followed in his own car.
It made sense, even if it wasn't the most efficient plan. If one of them needed to go after a
suspect or chase a lead, they wouldn't have to
drive all the way back to LaMar Pond and get
an extra car.

Ashley was just finishing her dinner when
they arrived. Her head turned sharply as they
entered the room, her short, dark hair brushing
her chin. The bruising that had been visible in
the crime-scene photos had healed, but she still
had a haunted look about her. She flinched as he
stepped into the room. He was glad that Parker
and Lizzy stayed in the waiting room. She was
jumpy enough without a crowd of strangers de-
scending upon her. Miles held out his badge as
he approached to question Ashley. He brought
Rebecca along because she had known Ashley
a little, and was very much a part of the inves-
tigation. Plus, he was reluctant to let her out of
his sight again. She slipped away far too often
for his peace of mind.

Approaching the hospital bed, he saw the way
Ashley's fists clenched.

"Miss Kline, I'm Officer Olsen from LaMar
Pond. I have some pictures to show you. One is
of the man I believe to be responsible for hurting you. If you're up to it?"

What would he say if she said no?

"Yes, I can look."

She pushed herself into a sitting position. Then she turned her focus on Rebecca for the first time. And gasped. "I remember her! She's the deaf girl that was taken with us. Rebecca."

Miles interpreted for Rebecca. "Yes. And it appears that the man who attacked you is going after the others who were with you that day."

Ashley's stiff posture deflated. "The others? Are they okay?"

He hadn't meant to open that can of worms. But since he had, he quickly related the events up to this point. Ashley's ashen complexion was wet with tears when he had finished.

"Let me see those pictures." She wiped the tears from her face.

He showed her Weller's image. "He did this?" She jabbed the picture with a long finger. "I know him! Brooke's cousin April is dating him!"

That gave him pause. "How do you know April?"

"Brooke and I have been in contact off and on since school. Last summer we were both invited to a former classmate's wedding. April was friends with the bride, too, so she was there, and he was her date."

Interesting.

"Was Holly there?"

She shook her head, and then her brow furrowed. She leaned her head to the side, thinking. "Now that I think of it, he was asking a lot of questions. But it was all done in a joking manner. It didn't feel like he was being nosy. But he was, wasn't he? He was getting info so he could grab us."

The real question was, did April know he was digging for information, or had she been duped, too? Chad could have targeted her deliberately, knowing she was close to Brooke, to give himself that connection and insight into their circle of friends. As for finding Rebecca... that would have been easy once April hired her. How had Rebecca ended up working at April's bookstore? That was a question he intended to find answers for.

"Why would he do this?"

The soft whisper brought him back to the conversation at hand.

"I don't have all the answers yet, but I do know that this man is Terry Gleason's half brother."

Ashley bit her knuckle. The pain in her gaze seared him. Rebecca brushed past him and held the other woman's hand. To his surprise, Ashley held tight. Or maybe it wasn't surprising. These two went through something devastating together.

He continued. "Jasmine's brother said that you and Jasmine had bullied and mocked Gleason in high school."

She snorted. "Yeah, he told the jury that, too. We never bullied him. He had asked both of us to a dance. We both said no, we had dates. His friends were the ones who teased him about it. They always made fun of him. Not us."

They didn't get too much more information out of her, but that was fine. It was enough to have a definite identification of who the killer was.

"I need to find out if April was involved in this."

Had April lured her into a trap?

She hated to think it was true, but had to admit it was a definite possibility. But April had always seemed so sincere. They hadn't been friends, but she had liked the woman.

"How did you start to work at the bookstore?" Miles. Dear Miles. He was fast becoming a steady rock in a crumbling world.

"April had asked Brooke if any of her friends needed a job, and Brooke had passed the information on to Holly, knowing that Holly sometimes had trouble holding down a job. She had something at that time, though, and knew I was job hunting, so she had asked if I could come and interview. She went in as my interpreter. April didn't want to hire me at first. She never said so, but I think the idea of working with a deaf woman intimidated her. But then later she called back and said the job was mine if I still wanted it. I did, so I started the next week."

"She probably had told Weller about you, and he realized who you were. In fact, it was probably his idea for her to ask Brooke to approach her old friends from school." He paused, rubbing his neck as he thought. "I think it's possible that he targeted April for information. She may not have had any idea what was happening. Or maybe she did. I have to find out."

When they entered the waiting room, Rebecca went to sit with her sister while the police officers made their plans. The whole situation was unreal. The planning that Chad Weller had done to carry out his vicious crimes was something she couldn't wrap her mind around. To plan the abductions and murders of four complete strangers! Even the thought of so much darkness made her shudder, as if she, too, had been tainted.

Lord, keep us safe. Keep us free from malice. Protect Miles as he goes after this man.

For he would go after him. She'd seen that expression. Miles would do whatever he could to keep the evil from touching her. Even if it meant he himself would be hurt.

And she loved him.

When had that happened?

She didn't like it, but accepted the truth. She was in love with Miles Olsen. And he wanted no part of any long-term relationship. Oh, sure, he'd kissed her. Her nerves buzzed thinking about that kiss. But that had been an emotional reaction to a narrow escape.

She longed for some gesture of affection now. Something to comfort her. She hadn't realized how much she had enjoyed those casual touches. But she feared he was going to start drawing away from her now. He didn't want any kind of emotional attachment.

The men approached them. She straightened, preparing herself for the next move in this dangerous game.

"You're both going to ride back with Parker." She clenched her hands to keep her protest in. "I will follow, then go and see if I can chat with April. Parker will take you and your sister back to Jess's house. You can stay there until I return. Please don't leave without me or Parker."

She nodded. A cold ache had started to grow inside her. Was this it?

Miles hesitated. Then, so quickly she had no

time to respond, he leaned in and kissed her. "Let's go."

She blinked. He'd kissed her. In front of his colleague and her sister. She bit the inside of her cheek, but the grin that started in her soul wouldn't be stopped. It stretched itself on her lips even as she pressed them together to keep it in.

Parker smirked after his colleague, but said nothing. Lizzy nudged her with an elbow. Rebecca felt her face heating up, but was too pleased to mind their teasing too much.

The drive back to LaMar Pond was uneventful. Rebecca fell asleep, and woke up in time to look back and see Miles turn toward the police station. Refusing to let fear gain control, she prayed the rest of the way back to Jess's house for his safety.

Parker pushed a button on the dashboard. Miles's name was there. He must have called. Was he okay? Every nerve stretched taut. She relaxed as she saw Parker laugh. He wouldn't laugh if Miles was hurt. But why had he called?

Lizzy was motioning to her in the mirror. Rebecca shifted in order to see her sister more clearly.

"It's your policeman." Rebecca blushed at that. She wished Miles was her policeman. "He called to check and see if we are fine. Mostly he wanted to know if you are fine."

She sat back, smiling. Miles was checking on her. Maybe he was missing her as much as she was missing him. That had to mean something, didn't it?

Her phone vibrated. April's number had come up on display. The text sent ice churning in her. Run as far as you can. Chad after you. He's a killer. I'm sorry. I didn't know. She showed it to Parker. He nodded and pulled off the road so he could read the text.

Parker said something. Lizzy tapped Rebecca's shoulder. "He said send it to Miles."

Rebecca nodded. But before she could forward the message, the windshield burst. Shocked, she dropped the phone on the floorboard. Parker slumped next to her, a red stain seeping over his shoulder. He'd been shot!

He was still awake, though. He reached for his gun, hitting the switch on the door as the face she'd now recognize anywhere loped toward them, a rifle in his hands.

He wasn't bothering with the ski mask. Which meant he knew they had his identity and he didn't care about hiding. None of them was safe anymore.

Lizzy pushed open the back passenger door

as Parker forced himself to stand and face the man coming toward them, his gun ready.

"He said run!" Lizzy signed to her.

Rebecca watched as Parker was thrown back against the car and slid to the ground.

Please don't be dead.

The killer was almost there. And there was no one to protect them.

SIXTEEN

Rebecca pushed open the door on her side. Parker had risked his life to save theirs, maybe he was already dead. She couldn't waste the chance.

She didn't expect to make it to safety. But maybe she could save her sister. She would willingly accept death if Lizzy could be saved. Her feet hit the pavement and she grabbed on to her sister's hand. Pulling the younger girl with her, they ran along the side of the road. If only there were woods to go to for cover!

But there were wide-open fields on both sides, a few cows and horses scattered in them. And now that they were out of the main center of LaMar Pond, there wasn't much by way of traffic or houses nearby, either.

A burning sensation stung her hip, causing her to stumble. Tears blurred her vision. She blinked them away. Now was not the time. She couldn't fall. Couldn't stop. Sucking in her breath and trying to ignore the agony, she continued pulling Lizzy along. Her hip burned with every step she took.

A chunk of gravel exploded in front of them. Another shot. She sidestepped the spot and kept moving. Another chunk flew up inches from them, showering gravel fragments on their dresses. She swerved to miss the new hole.

Lizzy tripped and fell, ripping her hand from Rebecca's grip.

Rebecca turned and reached out to Lizzy. It was too late. Chad Weller was already there, hauling her sister to her feet. He had thrown down the rifle. Was it empty? She didn't know. Either way, it didn't give her any peace. He drew a long, sharp knife from his belt and pushed the blade against the soft skin of Lizzy's throat. A small drop of blood appeared.

Rebecca understood the message. If she attempted to run, or made any wrong move, her sister would pay the price.

How could she save her now?

She couldn't. But God could. She prayed. Even as her breath grew shallow and her palms grew sweaty. Nausea struck her as they passed the police car. How she wanted to look and see if Parker was okay! But he was on the other side of the vehicle.

Weller continued to push the girls to his car,

parked farther up along the side of the road. He opened the back door, still holding the knife to Lizzy, and leaned in, emerging with a revolver.

A car was passing them. It slowed, faces gawking at the man holding a gun on two young women, one in an Amish dress. He scowled and aimed the revolver at the car. They got the message and raced away. Still scowling, he forced both girls into the back seat and tied their hands together. Slamming the door behind them, he got into the driver's seat and pulled away with enough force to make the sisters crash into each other. But where were they going?

It was all she could do not to vomit when they arrived at their destination.

Terry Gleason's old house. Chad Weller had bought his brother's old home. The memories flooded her panic-stricken mind. Images of being beaten, slapped, cut…all branded in her mind, impossible to forget.

She shook her head. Tried to focus on prayer. But her mind was too overwhelmed.

Please. Please.

Contradicting thoughts raced through her head. *Miles will come. But Miles is far away. The text from April had never been forwarded. It didn't matter. Miles always comes.*

She held on to her hope though it was as thin as a thread. But it helped her stay sane as her attacker pulled behind the house and parked near the back door. He didn't undo their hands. He hauled a dazed and terrified Lizzy out first then jerked his head at Rebecca. She climbed out on legs that felt like jelly, trembling so hard she could barely stand.

He sneered at her and said something. His sneer widened when she didn't answer. And with her hands bound, Lizzy couldn't tell her what he said.

Jerking his head again, he indicated that she needed to walk into the house. She did as she was told, her hope of being seen by a neighbor weakening with every step. She couldn't scream, either. Because there was a knife against her sister's throat again.

Opening the back door, she stepped into her own private nightmare. The house was clean but sparsely decorated. There were no personal touches like pictures or knickknacks.

Chad had bought the place only to torment his victims. He had no plans of making it his home. The cold-blooded way he'd gone about setting everything in its place chilled her.

Finally, he pushed them to a door. She froze. And shook her head vehemently. She was no longer seeing Chad Weller in front of her. She was seeing Terry Gleason, forcing them down the stairs into the basement. Chaining them up. Strangling Jasmine.

Something inside her broke as the image took control of her mind. She backed up and turned. Not to leave and abandon her sister. But in desperation to flee from her own memory.

A movement to her side. Lizzy had fallen, or had she been pushed? Her eyes were wide as she opened her mouth. Rebecca could tell she was screaming. A warning?

Chad stood with fury vibrating in every muscle of his body. He lashed out, his large fist catching Rebecca on the side of the face. She saw that she was falling toward the counter but couldn't move out of its way.

She was going to hit her head.

The pain lanced through her, then everything went black.

Miles wanted to call Parker, to check on Rebecca again. But he knew he couldn't. Not a second time. Parker had given him a hard time with the last call. But he couldn't shake the unease that had been brewing ever since he'd parted from the others.

Well, he knew what he needed to do. He needed to talk with Miss April Long and see if she could lead him to her boyfriend.

He really hoped she wasn't involved in all

this. His gut said no. Her concern over Brooke's disappearance struck him as genuine. And the car...

He tapped his hands on the steering wheel as he remembered the car driving by the Coles' house. Something had stopped the driver from shooting at them. April had walked outside to talk with them. And the driver had gone past.

Maybe Chad hadn't realized she'd be there? It was pretty bold for him to attack at the girl's home. But then, he had to have been feeling the cage closing in around him. Had to have known that his window of opportunity to fulfill his evil plan was closing.

Which was what scared Miles. The man was now acting out of desperation. Which meant he would be willing to take any opportunity to kill his victims.

Miles saw April's road and pulled in, quickly finding her house and parking. He radioed in that he had arrived at his destination. He got out of the car and strode up the path to the door, double time. He didn't have any time to waste.

Knocking briskly on the door, he blinked as the door swung in. It hadn't been shut. He called for backup, then drew his weapon and stepped inside. From where he stood, the place was a mess.

Someone had left in a hurry. Or had been

taken. Things were overturned, as if there had been a struggle, and there was blood on the floor.

Dialing the chief's number, he gave him a rundown. When the chief gave him permission to proceed with caution, he stepped carefully inside, hoping he wouldn't find a body.

He didn't. He did find a suitcase, half-packed in a haphazard fashion and abandoned, open, on the bed.

She'd been leaving. Running away, from the look of it.

And she'd been caught before she could finish.

Voices outside. Backup had arrived.

The scene was processed, pictures taken. There was a picture taken at a wedding. Brooke, Ashley and April all smiling, arms around each other. Brooke was in the center. It was heartbreaking, the joy on all three young faces.

And a man with revenge on his mind had deliberately set out to use one of them to get to the other two—and two others, as well. They needed to find Brooke and April fast.

He was heading back to the station to do the paperwork when Parker texted. Weller attacked. I'm shot, ambulance on the way. He has girls.

Miles stopped breathing. No! How had this happened? If anything happened to Rebecca...

What could he do? He arrived at the station, ran into Chief Kennedy's office and showed him the text, not trusting himself to speak. The chief didn't mess around. Every available officer was brought in and a search began.

"Olsen." It was Lieutenant Tucker.

"Sir." He didn't have time to chat now. He had a woman to save. Some of his struggle must have shown on his face, because Tucker's own face softened. Which freaked him out a little.

"Miles." And that freaked him out more. Because the lieutenant never called him by his first name at work. "I know what you're going through. We have all seen how hard you've fallen for Miss Miller. And we're behind you. We won't leave any lead unchecked. And we'll help you bring her back."

Miles looked away until his eyes stopped stinging. "I appreciate it, Jace."

And he meant it. The officer had clearly forgiven him for his past actions. And now he was offering more than support. This was friendship. And he needed it, was happy to accept it. Jace nodded and left him. Miles headed back out to his own car to begin the search. But where to begin?

His ringtone went off. It was the chief. He tapped his watch. "Olsen here."

"Someone just called the station. They heard

what sounded like screaming at the house that Terry Gleason's family used to own. It had been sold again recently. They said the new owner is a young man who keeps to himself, so they called it in."

"I'm on my way. Have all available officers and an ambulance meet me at that location. Tell them not to go in hot. We don't want to lose the advantage of surprise. Who knows what he'll do if he hears us coming."

"Take care, Olsen. Wait for backup before you go in."

"I'll be careful, Chief. And if I can wait, I will."

SEVENTEEN

Consciousness slowly returned.

With it, came pain. Rebecca forced her swollen eyelids open, blinking against the grainy texture that scratched her eyes. Was she on the floor? Yes, her cheek was resting on cold cement, and the scent of dust filled her nostrils and coated her throat.

Gingerly, she sat up. The room swayed briefly. It was dim, and cold, but there was enough light coming in from a single light bulb attached to the ceiling to get a vague impression of her surroundings. Half a dozen cement posts ran from the floor to the ceiling, each about six inches in diameter. She remembered the half-circle windows around the ceiling. Terry Gleason's basement. The furniture was restricted to one couch against a wall and two end tables.

Memory came rushing back. Lizzy! Where was her sister? She scrabbled up on her hands and knees and tried to stand. That's when she noticed the shackles. Her left leg was shackled, and the chain was bolted to one of the posts. Just like before. At least her hands were free this time. Or were they left this way to taunt her?

The ability to breathe was getting difficult. Fear and anxiety were clawing their way up her throat, working against her lungs, blocking out the air. She couldn't pass out! She had to find her sister!

A movement to her left caught her eye. Someone was sitting against the wall, shackled to a post just like she was. It was Lizzy. Relief coursed through her, allowing her to breathe again. Lizzy was dazed, but she didn't appear to have been hurt. She stared at Rebecca, and tears started to flow down her smooth cheeks.

"It's okay, Lizzy. God knows we are here. And Miles will search for us."

"How will he find us? No one knows where we are."

Rebecca did her best to reassure Lizzy. "It doesn't matter. Miles has been working very hard finding answers. He won't give up. You don't know him like I do. He will keep looking."

Her heart ached at the thought. Miles. Sweet Miles. He would search relentlessly until she was found. She knew that. What would happen to him if she was hurt? Would he carry that burden in his heart the way he did with his sister?

Dear Lord, help Miles find us. And help him let go of his remorse. Lord, I love him. Let me have the chance to tell him that.

Had her brother's wedding only been this morning?

Doubt crept into her mind. The idea that Chad would buy this house had never occurred to them. How was Miles supposed to find her?

Have faith, she reminded herself. *God is in control. No matter how dark or hopeless the situation, He is in control.*

"Someone else is here," Lizzy signed. "Another woman."

Rebecca glanced around carefully. Too much movement made her head throb. She hadn't even noticed the third woman, chained on the opposite side of the room. Even without seeing the woman's face, she knew who it was under the curtain of short, curly blond hair. Brooke. And Brooke was obviously hurt. Her arm hung at an odd angle, and there was blood on it.

She had disappeared several days before Rebecca and Lizzy were taken. Chad seemed to be changing his pattern. Was she still alive? And why had he taken all three of them? He'd taken Ashley and Holly one at a time.

A bright light flared to life. Rebecca and Lizzy both shrank bank, blinking their eyes as the brightness struck them. It took a few minutes for her gaze to focus on the figures coming toward her. Figures?

For there were two people. One seemed to be pushing the other. Her vision cleared. She watched, heart thudding in her throat, as Chad pushed April into the room ahead of him, and shoved her down on the couch. The force of the shove caused her to fall, her ankle wrenching. Her face twisted, and she opened her mouth as if she was speaking. No. Not speaking. Crying out. Although Rebecca wasn't sure if it was in fear or pain. Probably both. But why had Chad taken her? She wasn't part of the original group. Nor had she been with either Brooke or Rebecca, as Lizzy had been. Something wasn't making sense.

Chad scowled down at the weeping woman on the couch, disgust crawling across his face. When he abruptly switched his attention to Rebecca, she froze. The pure malice she encountered made her want to crawl out of her own skin. She shivered and inched away from him as far as the chain around her ankle would allow.

Until he turned and fixed that horrible gaze on Lizzy.

Hot, liquid rage burned through her chest, hazing over in her mind and burning away the fear as he kicked the young Amish girl. Pain flashed across Lizzy's face. Her mouth opened, her cry of pain a silent dart into Rebecca's heart. Rebecca lunged forward. That chain stopped her before she could get anywhere near the monster standing in the middle of the room. He sneered, and snarled at Lizzy. She shook her head fiercely. Until he said something else. It didn't seem possible but Lizzy paled even more. Tears streamed down her cheeks as she signed to her sister.

"He says he will kill you if I don't tell you what he is saying."

He will kill us anyway, if he can. Rebecca didn't say the words. This was hard enough without scaring her little sister even more. *Please, Lord. Save us. Send Miles.*

Chad continued hurling words at Lizzy, watching their effect on Rebecca as the younger girl silently, haltingly, signed them to her sister.

"He says this is all your fault. I will die, and it is your fault. You and your friends. He knows because he found where his brother had been after he died. He had been looking for him for a long time. Terry had told people that Jasmine and Ashley had been part of a group that had bullied him in high school. That was why they needed to be taught a lesson. Then at the trial, you and your friends continued to torment him. Terry went to jail, and died there. Because of you and your friends this man was denied a real reunion with the only family he had left."

"But Holly and I were never part of the group that made fun of his brother."

Lizzy interpreted, and got another kick from Chad.

Rebecca held in the protests gurgling up inside her. The pressure was intense. The last thing she wanted was for this man to turn his vitriol on her sister.

He continued talking.

"He says to stop lying—that he knows better than to believe anything you'd say. He says that he has been planning this for a long time. He met April, and realized that she had gone to high school with the other girls. When she mentioned her cousin Brooke, he knew she was his link to all of you. He dated April for two months before it paid off. She was invited to a wedding and brought him as her date—he met Ashley and Brooke there. He convinced April to hire someone at the store so they could spend more time together. He convinced her to hire you when..." Lizzy's signs slowed, and then paused. Rebecca understood. She didn't want to tell her what April had really thought about her when she'd applied for the job. It didn't matter. She knew.

But why was he going after April now? Rebecca glanced at the woman on the couch without thinking, then whipped her eyes back to the man towering before her. He sneered again. It seemed that whatever affection he'd had for April was gone.

"She is weak," he said, pointing to April. Lizzy's hands trembled as she continued to sign. "I thought I had found someone I could trust. But she found out what I was doing. She tried to break it off with me, and I knew she planned on going to the police. That's your fault, too."

He advanced three steps toward Rebecca. Shrinking back was instinctive. "If you had died in the store like you were supposed to, she would never have known. You have cost me my brother and my girlfriend. And now, the police even have my picture broadcast on the news. You don't deserve an easy death. None of you do. Not after all you have cost me."

April suddenly moved, jumping up from the couch and leaping toward him, her hands curled like claws. She was no match for him. Enraged, he caught her and slammed her back against the wall, inches away from where Rebecca was chained, his hands at his former girlfriend's throat.

He was choking her!

He was focused on April, not paying attention to Rebecca's movements. And Rebecca was close enough to reach him now. With a strength she never knew she possessed, Rebecca hurtled herself at his unprotected back and grabbed on to him, her hands clawing and scratching at his face, at his neck.

Chad released April and swiped Rebecca from his back. April fell in a heap to the ground. All his rage was fixed on Rebecca now. He dragged her up by her hair and pressed her back against the wall. He leaned his face in close. His breath washed over her. Stomach turning, she struggled. He was too strong. His hands reached up and closed around her neck. She scratched at his hands. Remembered how she had escaped before and tried to gouge out his eyes. He dodged out of the way.

She was going to die. Her mind grew blurry. Miles. He was going to be too late.

Miles pushed his way past the broken gate blocking the path and raced up the creaky stairs to the front porch, his gun in his hand. He prayed that backup would get there fast. Somewhere inside the house, he could hear a young girl screaming. Lizzy. Which could mean that Rebecca was in dire straits even as he opened the battered door.

Lord, protect her. Shield her.

His mind wasn't capable of stringing together

more than that. So he repeated it, knowing that the God of all would understand what was in his heart.

He probably should have waited for another cruiser to arrive. That would have been the safe, responsible thing to do. Moreover, it was what his chief had directly ordered him to do, and doing otherwise could have serious consequences for his career. But he couldn't take the chance of being too late. Not when Rebecca's life was at risk. Nothing was more important than getting to the woman he loved right now. Not even his job. If he saved her, but lost his job, he would consider himself blessed.

Crashing through the front door, he followed the screaming and noises. They were coming from below. The basement. He attempted to be cautious as he hurried down the basement stairs, trying to keep his noise to a minimum. Not that anyone would be able to hear him over Lizzy's screaming. And another woman was groaning. Brooke?

Jumping down the last three steps, he burst in on a horrific scene. Lizzy and a blonde woman he recognized as Brooke were both chained to posts. Lizzy had pulled herself as close to Chad as she could, screaming and trying to reach him, tears pouring down her face. The woman moaning on the floor was barely recognizable as April. Her neck was bruising. As if she had been strangled.

And Rebecca!

A red haze of rage misted over his brain as he saw Chad's long fingers around her throat. With a roar, Miles charged at him and knocked him away from the woman he loved. She toppled to the floor. Was she alive?

For a suspended moment, his heart stopped beating, and he couldn't breathe. Until she started to move and cough. It was a weak, wheezy sound. But it meant his Rebecca was alive. He hadn't lost her.

He'd turned his back on Chad too long. The other man charged at him, a knife in his hand. He sliced at Miles's arm. Miles jumped back out of the way just in time.

The two men circled in the traditional fighting stance. Miles knew he couldn't risk shooting. Not with all the women in the room.

The other man grinned, an angry leer filled with malice. He probably assumed that without his gun, Miles was weak. His face grew cocky. He maneuvered closer and closer, swinging the sharp knife in front of him. He was taunting Miles.

Miles let him.

The anger settled, cooling and hardening into fierce determination. Calmness filled him. He sent up a prayer of gratitude. God had prepared him for this day, although he hadn't understood at the time. God had given him skills that made him capable of defending himself, and the four helpless women, from the man dancing before him.

His fear vanished. He was, after all, a black belt.

Chad lunged, knife swinging.

Miles was ready. He stepped into the charge, and kicked. The knife dropped and skidded across the cement floor. For the briefest instant, Chad was still, speechless. Then he howled and charged again, his head low and arms out. He intended to tackle Miles to the floor. Miles bent and scooped his arms under Chad's, bringing his hands behind the other man's back. Chad squirmed, but couldn't break loose. One, two times Miles thrust his knee into the other man's stomach.

Chad buckled.

In an instant, Miles had him on his stomach and was clapping handcuffs on him, reciting his Miranda rights.

The front door slammed.

"Olsen!"

"In the basement, Jackson! I have four women down here who require medical care."

The rush of footsteps thumping down the stairs was one of the best sounds he had ever heard.

As the paramedics and police swarmed into the basement, Miles went over and kneeled by Rebecca. Her eyes were open. She blinked, then narrowed her eyes on his face.

"You came," she signed, a tear trickling down her dusty cheek. "I knew you would come. I was afraid it wouldn't be in time."

A sobbing to his left made him pause. April was having a meltdown as the paramedic checked her over. "I didn't mean to help him! I didn't know what he was doing until it was too late!"

What?

Rebecca patted his knee. He switched his attention back to her instantly. "She was his girlfriend. He used her to get to us. When she found out, she tried to break up with him. She sent me a warning text before, when Sergeant Parker was driving us home. It just came too late—we were attacked before I could send it to you."

He wiped the tear from her face, then realized he was fighting back his own tears. "I don't know what I would have down if I had lost you."

She smiled. He sucked in a breath. And sat down, hard, shaking. "I love you. You know that, right? When I knew you were in trouble, nothing else mattered. Not my job, my past, nothing. Only you."

"I love you, too. I am so grateful that God

created a man so special, and let me have him in my life." She stopped signing, a frown touching her face. "Your job? Will you lose your job? Why?"

Miles had been aware on some level of Seth, who was part of the team of paramedics, telling the chief the less personal details of the signed conversation, including the part about April.

"He's worried he might lose his job because he didn't follow protocol today when he learned you were in danger. He put you first." Seth signed the answer to Rebecca for Miles. It was a good thing, because she was clinging to his hands. The chief looked at Miles. Not, Miles was glad to see, with anger or disappointment.

"Officer Olsen, I am rather proud of your deportment on this case." Miles couldn't help the way his jaw dropped. The shock nearly knocked him over.

The ambulance crew started to load up the women on stretchers. Lizzy insisted on walking, as soon as they had freed her. April and Brooke were in no shape to walk, though. Neither was Rebecca. All he wanted was to go with her. The chief motioned for him to stay back. He obeyed, but wasn't happy about it.

Chief Kennedy chuckled. "Easy, officer. This will only take a moment. Then you can go to the hospital and be with your girl."

Miles felt himself flushing. He'd been pretty obvious about his feelings, he guessed.

"Officer Olsen, I want you to know that I believe you did the correct thing."

His head shot up. "Sir? I disobeyed a direct order. You told me to wait for backup. And I didn't."

"I know. And normally I'd be furious with you. But if you hadn't, at least one of those women, if not more, would have died. Your actions and quick thinking saved the lives of four women. And you managed to capture a vicious killer, alive. He will go to jail, and those women will be able to go on with their lives, instead of constantly looking over their shoulders. Well done."

"Thank you, sir!" He couldn't wait to go to the hospital and tell Rebecca!

"Oh, and Miles—" the chief paused at the base of the stairs "—I think it's time we reviewed your record. I think you've earned a promotion. Don't you?"

Whistling that same TV show theme song, the chief started up the stairs. Miles stared after him a moment, unable to believe his ears. Then a grin split his face. He all but ran out to his car to go see Rebecca.

Of course, once he arrived at the hospital, he had to wait for her to be seen by a doctor. When he was finally able to see her, she was getting ready to go.

"They aren't keeping you overnight?" he signed, surprised.

"No." She grinned and winked. "I can go anytime."

"Where will you go?"

"I can't go back to my apartment. I'm going to move out of there. But Seth invited me back to his place."

That was a relief. Even with the danger gone, he hated to think of her in that apartment she had shared with Holly, knowing the sad memories it would bring back. "Can I give you a ride?"

She hesitated. "Maybe. First, did you mean what you said in the basement?"

"Yes," he signed without missing a beat. "I love you."

She sighed. A sigh that seemed to come from deep in her soul. Her eyes closed. But only for a moment. When she opened them again, she graced him with a mischievous smirk, one that took his breath away. "Then why haven't you kissed me yet?"

He could do nothing about the grin that spread from his heart and across his face. Or about the way his entire being hummed with love for this bright woman. "I have no idea."

And because there was no good reason not to, and being the intelligent man that he was, he pulled her gently into his arms and kissed her.

EPILOGUE

One month later

It had started to snow while she was inside. Fluffy white flakes drifted down. Already, the layer on the ground was two inches deep. She grinned and stuck out her tongue to catch a cold flake. She loved winter. Thanksgiving was next week. Miles had invited her to spend the evening with him at his grandparents' house. His father would even be there. Rebecca was nervous to meet him, but she knew Miles would be there to support her. As he always did.

Rebecca cast a glance at her watch as she made her way to where her car was parked. She felt confident that she had done well on the test. She'd get her scores back sometime after Christmas. If all went well, she would be able to take the performance portion of the exam in the spring or summer.

Right now, though, she was running late for

her dinner date with Miles. Just thinking of the love of her life brought a smile to her face. They'd been dating for a month now. Maybe it was too soon by society standards, but she knew he was the man she wanted to spend the rest of her life with. When would she ever find another man who understood her so well, who made her heart race and loved God as much as she did?

She was going to see Miles tonight, in fact. Her parents had invited them over to their house for dinner. At first, she'd been tempted to re-schedule. She and Miles had a lot to celebrate. His chief had been very pleased with Miles's work on her case. In fact, he had just been rein-stated as a sergeant. But, like the sensitive man he was, he had convinced her to accept the in-vitation. It would mean so much to them.

Sending a prayer of thanksgiving to her Fa-ther in Heaven, she searched through her over-large purse for her cell phone to send Miles a text. Behind schedule. Leaving now.

A moment later, her phone vibrated. That's ok. I'm behind schedule 2. Meet you at your par-ents' house? Love u.

Fine. Love u 2.

It took her almost an hour to go home, shower and change, and get ready to leave. As she was finishing getting ready, her gaze in the mirror caught on the small earrings in her ears. She'd gotten her ears pierced soon after she and Lizzy had been rescued. Miles had gone with her and had held her hand as they put the piercing gun to her ears.

It was more than jewelry to her. It was a physical sign that she knew who she was and which world she belonged in.

She hesitated. Should she take them out before going to her parents' house? She pondered, then pressed her lips together. No. Her parents knew her choices. And they accepted them and loved her. They were generous people who wouldn't let this effect their relationship.

The earrings stayed in.

She drove to the farmhouse near Spartansburg, her excitement growing with every turn in the road. Soon, she'd see Miles. They hadn't been able to see each other for two days because of work schedules. Funny how long two days could be!

Pulling into the driveway, she noted his Jeep was already there. She bounced out of her car and nearly ran up the stairs. He met her at the door. She knew why. Once inside, there would be no hello kiss. Not with her parents watching. But here, out of their sight...

Miles let the door close behind him and

pulled her gently into his arms. She snuggled closer, feeling like everything was right in her world again. He bent and kissed her slowly, letting her know how much he'd missed her the past few days.

"I missed you," he signed when the kiss ended.

She sighed. Bliss. "Missed you, back. Two days is a very long time."

"Forever," he agreed.

In sync, they moved into the house. Her *mam* hugged her, the sparkle in her eyes letting them know she wasn't fooled. She knew why they'd met outside.

Rebecca was too happy to be embarrassed.

It was a perfect evening. Her *mam* and *dat* were pleased to see their oldest daughter. They didn't so much sign as gesture, letting Miles take care of facilitating the communication. She didn't mind. They were trying, and they were showing their care and love in every gesture.

It wasn't until the meal was almost finished that Rebecca got the hint that something else was going on. Her normally calm father seemed a little flustered, and her mother's smile grew more pronounced, even though she kept putting her napkin to her mouth to hide it.

And Miles? Since when had he become clumsy? He'd dropped his fork twice. The second time he picked it up, he gave her *dat* a small nod. Like a signal.

Uh-oh.

What was going on?

Her father reached over and patted her hand. She looked at him, suspicion growing.

He started to gesture, then stopped. He rose and went to grab some paper and a pencil. And began to write.

Rebecca, my daughter. I want to tell you this myself. I do not sign, so I will write. Miles came to talk to us. He said it was an Englisch custom. He asked us for our blessing to marry our beautiful daughter.

Her breath stalled and her heart quickened. Was this really happening?

Her *dat* continued.

We love you, and would be very happy to have him as our son. We told him yes. He has our blessing. So do you.

She stopped fighting the tears and let them fall. Miles stood up from his chair and moved to her side. He kneeled down on one knee before her, and began to sign. Straight ASL. She understood the message. This moment was just for her. They could repeat it for her family later.

"Rebecca, I love you with all my heart. You are strong, and beautiful in every way. You make my life complete. We have not been dating long, but these past two days without you have been very lonely. Please, marry me?"

Her heart was full. "Yes. I love you so much. I will marry you!"

His eyes glinted. He blinked. Then reached into his pocket to pull out a ring. It was simplicity itself.

This man truly understood her.

Holding out her left hand, she didn't care that it trembled. It should tremble. With joy and hope. Her life was changing forever.

She'd spent too much time holding her heart back. Now, she was giving it freely to this man.

He slid the ring on her hand. Then, even with her parents watching, he leaned in and kissed her softly. She smiled against his lips, the promise of the future bright in her heart.

* * * * *

*If you loved this book, don't miss the first
heart-stopping Amish adventure
from Dana R. Lynn's*
AMISH COUNTRY JUSTICE *series:*

PLAIN TARGET

*Find more great reads at
www.LoveInspired.com*

Dear Reader,

I am so happy to be able to share Miles and Rebecca's story with you! This is the second book in my Amish Country Justice series, and it was both a joy and a challenge to write.

When I first started writing *Presumed Guilty* in 2014, Miles was one of those characters who tugged at my heart. He had so many issues to reconcile, and had gotten off track a bit. He had lost his way. Yet, God was with him. And I knew I wanted to write his story, to show that he had changed and found redemption. I was touched by the readers who wrote to me asking for his story.

Rebecca was first introduced in *Plain Target*. She was so much fun to write about! She had been through so much, yet still managed to keep God at the heart of her life.

I hope you enjoyed Miles and Rebecca's story. I have one more to go in this trilogy, and I am really excited about it. It has been amazing following my characters into the Amish community.

Thank you for journeying with me. I love to hear from readers. You can email me at

WriterDanaLynn@gmail.com. Or visit me online at www.danarlynn.com. I am also on Facebook and Twitter (@DanaRLynn).

Blessings,
Dana R. Lynn

Get 2 Free Books,
Plus 2 Free Gifts—
just for trying the Reader Service!

YES! Please send me 2 FREE Love Inspired® Romance novels and my 2 FREE mystery gifts (gifts are worth about $10 retail). After receiving them, if I don't wish to receive any more books, I can return the shipping statement marked "cancel." If I don't cancel, I will receive 6 brand-new novels every month and be billed just $5.24 for the regular-print edition or $5.74 each for the larger-print edition in the U.S., or $5.74 each for the regular-print edition or $6.24 each for the larger-print edition in Canada. That's a saving of at least 13% off the cover price. It's quite a bargain! Shipping and handling is just 50¢ per book in the U.S. and 75¢ per book in Canada.* I understand that accepting the 2 free books and gifts places me under no obligation to buy anything. I can always return a shipment and cancel at any time. The free books and gifts are mine to keep no matter what I decide.

Please check one:

☐ Love Inspired Romance Regular-Print
   (105/305 IDN GLWW)

☐ Love Inspired Romance Larger-Print
   (122/322 IDN GLWW)

Name	(PLEASE PRINT)	
Address		Apt. #
City	State/Province	Zip/Postal Code

Signature (if under 18, a parent or guardian must sign)

Mail to the **Reader Service:**

IN U.S.A.: P.O. Box 1341, Buffalo, NY 14240-8531
IN CANADA: P.O. Box 603, Fort Erie, Ontario L2A 5X3

Want to try two free books from another line?
Call 1-800-873-8635 today or visit www.ReaderService.com.

*Terms and prices subject to change without notice. Prices do not include applicable taxes. Sales tax applicable in N.Y. Canadian residents will be charged applicable taxes. Offer not valid in Quebec. This offer is limited to one order per household. Books received may not be as shown. Not valid for current subscribers to Love Inspired Romance books. All orders subject to approval. Credit or debit balances in a customer's account(s) may be offset by any other outstanding balance owed by or to the customer. Please allow 4 to 6 weeks for delivery. Offer available while quantities last.

Your Privacy—The Reader Service is committed to protecting your privacy. Our Privacy Policy is available online at www.ReaderService.com or upon request from the Reader Service.

We make a portion of our mailing list available to reputable third parties that offer products we believe may interest you. If you prefer that we not exchange your name with third parties, or if you wish to clarify or modify your communication preferences, please visit us at www.ReaderService.com/consumerschoice or write to us at Reader Service Preference Service, P.O. Box 9062, Buffalo, NY 14240-9062. Include your complete name and address.

LI17R2

Get 2 Free Books,

Plus 2 Free Gifts—

just for trying the
Reader Service!

YES! Please send me 2 FREE Harlequin® Heartwarming™ Larger-Print novels and my 2 FREE mystery gifts (gifts worth about $10 retail). After receiving them, if I don't wish to receive any more books, I can return the shipping statement marked "cancel." If I don't cancel, I will receive 4 brand-new larger-print novels every month and be billed just $5.49 per book in the U.S. or $6.24 per book in Canada. That's a savings of at least 19% off the cover price. It's quite a bargain! Shipping and handling is just 50¢ per book in the U.S. and 75¢ per book in Canada.* I understand that accepting the 2 free books and gifts places me under no obligation to buy anything. I can always return a shipment and cancel at any time. The free books and gifts are mine to keep no matter what I decide.

161/361 IDN GLWT

Name	(PLEASE PRINT)	
Address		Apt. #
City	State/Prov.	Zip/Postal Code

Signature (if under 18, a parent or guardian must sign)

Mail to the **Reader Service:**
IN U.S.A.: P.O. Box 1341, Buffalo, NY 14240-8531
IN CANADA: P.O. Box 603, Fort Erie, Ontario L2A 5X3

Want to try two free books from another line?
Call 1-800-873-8635 today or visit www.ReaderService.com.

* Terms and prices subject to change without notice. Prices do not include applicable taxes. Sales tax applicable in N.Y. Canadian residents will be charged applicable taxes. Offer not valid in Quebec. This offer is limited to one order per household. Books received may not be as shown. Not valid for current subscribers to Harlequin Heartwarming Larger-Print books. All orders subject to approval. Credit or debit balances in a customer's account(s) may be offset by any other outstanding balance owed by or to the customer. Please allow 4 to 6 weeks for delivery. Offer available while quantities last.

Your Privacy—The Reader Service is committed to protecting your privacy. Our Privacy Policy is available online at www.ReaderService.com or upon request from the Reader Service.

We make a portion of our mailing list available to reputable third parties that offer products we believe may interest you. If you prefer that we not exchange your name with third parties, or if you wish to clarify or modify your communication preferences, please visit us at www.ReaderService.com/consumerschoice or write to us at Reader Service Preference Service, P.O. Box 9062, Buffalo, NY 14240-9062. Include your complete name and address.

HOMETOWN HEARTS ♡

YES! Please send me **The Hometown Hearts Collection** in Larger Print. This collection begins with 3 FREE books and 2 FREE gifts in the first shipment. Along with my 3 free books, I'll also get the next 4 books from the Hometown Hearts Collection, in LARGER PRINT, which I may either return and owe nothing, or keep for the low price of $4.99 U.S./ $5.89 CDN each plus $2.99 for shipping and handling per shipment*. If I decide to continue, about once a month for 8 months I will get 6 or 7 more books, but will only need to pay for 4. That means 2 or 3 books in every shipment will be FREE! If I decide to keep the entire collection, I'll have paid for only 32 books because 19 books are FREE! I understand that accepting the 3 free books and gifts places me under no obligation to buy anything. I can always return a shipment and cancel at any time. My free books and gifts are mine to keep no matter what I decide.

262 HCN 3432 462 HCN 3432

Name	(PLEASE PRINT)	
Address		Apt. #
City	State/Prov.	Zip/Postal Code

Signature (if under 18, a parent or guardian must sign)

Mail to the **Reader Service:**

IN U.S.A.: P.O. Box 1867, Buffalo, NY. 14240-1867
IN CANADA: P.O. Box 609, Fort Erie, Ontario L2A 5X3

* Terms and prices subject to change without notice. Prices do not include applicable taxes. Sales tax applicable in NY. Canadian residents will be charged applicable taxes. This offer is limited to one order per household. All orders subject to approval. Credit or debit balances in a customer's account(s) may be offset by any other outstanding balance owed by or to the customer. Please allow 4 to 6 weeks for delivery. Offer available while quantities last. Offer not available to Quebec residents.

Your Privacy—The Reader Service is committed to protecting your privacy. Our Privacy Policy is available online at www.ReaderService.com or upon request from the Reader Service.

We make a portion of our mailing list available to reputable third parties that offer products we believe may interest you. If you prefer that we not exchange your name with third parties, or if you wish to clarify or modify your communication preferences, please visit us at www.ReaderService.com/consumerchoice or write to us at Reader Service Preference Service, P.O. Box 9062, Buffalo, NY. 14240-9062. Include your complete name and address.

Get 2 Free Books,
Plus 2 Free Gifts—
just for trying the Reader Service!

Love Inspired HISTORICAL

READERSERVICE.COM

Manage your account online!
- Review your order history
- Manage your payments
- Update your address

*We've designed the
Reader Service website
just for you.*

Enjoy all the features!
- Discover new series available to you, and read excerpts from any series.
- Respond to mailings and special monthly offers.
- Browse the Bonus Bucks catalog and online-only exculsives.
- Share your feedback.

Visit us at:
ReaderService.com

RS16R